"I'm not out of my depth!"

"Oh, yes, my dear Angelica, you most certainly are," Luke Cunningham murmured. "Why else should you be so determined to fight me every inch of the way?"

"You're quite wrong...this really isn't a good idea. Lust may be a reason to get married, but it's not enough!"

Luke shrugged and gave a harsh, sardonic laugh.

"As far as I'm concerned, it will certainly do to be going on with!"

MARY LYONS was born in Toronto, Canada, moving to live permanently in England when she was six, although she still proudly maintains her Canadian citizenship. Having married and raised four children, her life nowadays is relatively peaceful—unlike her earlier years when she worked as a radio announcer, reviewed books and, for a time, lived in a turbulent area of the Middle East. She still enjoys a bit of excitement, combining romance with action, humor and suspense in her books whenever possible.

Books by Mary Lyons

HARLEQUIN PRESENTS
1499—DARK AND DANGEROUS
1610—SILVER LADY
1633—LOVE IS THE KEY
1781—YULETIDE BRIDE

Don't miss any of our special offers. Write to us at the following address for information on our newest releases.

Harlequin Reader Service
U.S.: 3010 Walden Ave., P.O. Box 1325, Buffalo, NY 14269
Canadian: P.O. Box 609, Fort Erie, Ont. L2A 5X3

MARY LYONS

LYONS

It Started With A Kiss

Harlequin Books

TORONTO • NEW YORK • LONDON
AMSTERDAM • PARIS • SYDNEY • HAMBURG
STOCKHOLM • ATHENS • TOKYO • MILAN
MADRID • WARSAW • BUDAPEST • AUCKLAND

ISBN 0-373-11801-5

IT STARTED WITH A KISS

First North American Publication 1996.

Copyright © 1994 by Mary Lyons.

Printed in U.S.A.

CHAPTER ONE

'YES, I'm sorry. Yes, I *do* realise that I'm giving you very short notice.'

Angelica sighed, brushing a tired hand through her long ash-blonde hair and grimacing at the irritation in the voice on the other end of the telephone.

'Look, I understand your problems, David,' she broke in hurriedly. 'But it's hardly *my* fault if the men who've been replacing some tiles on the roof completely forgot to put a tarpaulin over a large hole when they left work yesterday. And after that heavy rainstorm last night...well, I'm now looking up at what's left of my bedroom ceiling; there's water and chunks of old plaster covering most of the floor, and since about one o'clock this morning Betty and I have been rushing around with buckets and mops, just praying that all the other bedroom ceilings wouldn't cave in as well!'

'Yes, I can see——'

'Most of the carpets and bedding are completely soaked—not to mention *all* the clothes in my wardrobe, which seems to have taken the brunt of the deluge,' Angelica continued with a heavy sigh. 'Goodness knows how we're going to get everything dried out. Honestly, David, it's been an absolute *nightmare*! Even if we keep on working flat out, it's going to take ages to clear up the mess. On top of which I'm now in the middle of an almighty row with the roofers; one of the trustees, who lives near by, has already been moaning away on the phone, and——'

'OK, OK,' David Webster interjected quickly. 'Although why you want to keep on living in that huge barn of a house, crammed full of dusty old paintings and goodness knows what else, beats me.'

'Because it's always been my home—and I love it!' Angelica retorted, well aware that most of her friends thought she was completely crazy. 'Oh, come on,' she pleaded. 'You know all about the situation I'm in regarding the trust. Right?'

'I'm sorry—I didn't mean to sound so unsympathetic,' he told her gruffly. 'But it still doesn't solve my problem. How am I supposed, at a moment's notice, to find someone to take your place? I can just see all those people milling around outside the Houses of Parliament, and——'

'Relax!' she said quickly. 'There's no need to worry. I've already phoned Greg, and he's quite happy to swap his tour for mine. We've arranged that he'll be doing my *Historic Westminster* walk this morning, while I take over his *Famous Square Mile* tour through the City later on this afternoon. OK?'

'Yes...I suppose that's better than nothing,' David grumbled. 'I'm not worried about Greg—he could find his way around London with his eyes shut. But you've never done that particular route before. In fact,' he added with a gloomy sigh, 'I'll bet that what you know about the London Stock Exchange, for instance, can be written on the back of a small postage stamp!'

'Don't worry—I'll manage,' Angelica told him firmly, quickly putting down the phone before her boss could think of any more objections.

She was very fond of David Webster, an old friend from her days at university. But why did he always have to be quite so pessimistic? Everyone knew that business life was tough these days. However, his agency, Footsteps in Time, which organised and ran various walking tours of London, appeared to be doing very well. Having been one of his part-time guides for the past two years, Angelica really loved showing foreign visitors and tourists the odd, unusual aspects of London. Especially since much of the city's ancient past lay hidden behind narrow, twisting streets and alleys— virtually inaccessible by car, but ideal for a leisurely stroll on foot.

Her thoughts were interrupted as her old nanny and present housekeeper, Betty Roberts, bustled into the room. Standing with her arms akimbo, the plump woman glared up at the large hole in the ceiling, and then at the oil paintings which had been so hastily pulled down from the walls, their gilt frames casually piled high on a dry part of the floor, as if ready for a bonfire.

'Well, this room is a right shambles, and no mistake! Your grandmother was always so proud of this house. She'd surely turn in her grave if she could see this mess,' Betty muttered angrily.

'I know,' Angelica agreed, sighing heavily as she surveyed the chaotic scene. 'It's really depressing. There's so much to clear up that I simply can't seem to think exactly where to begin.'

'You look tired to death,' the older woman told her brusquely. 'Why don't you pop down to the kitchen and make a nice pot of tea? I reckon that we could both do with a cuppa.'

Realising that Betty was right, and that they both needed a break from cleaning up the storm damage, Angelica slowly made her way down the flights of stairs to the kitchen in the basement.

Hardly touched since the house was first built in 1723, the large cavernous kitchen still possessed an ancient black cooking range, which was still in working order—although Betty had long ago badgered Angelica's grandmother into providing a modern, up-to-date cooker and refrigerator. Together with a tall Welsh dresser, holding row upon row of copper bowls and saucepans, and an enormous scrubbed pine table surrounded by comfortable, high-backed chairs, the old kitchen was a warm and cosy room, which had hardly altered since the days of her great-great-grand-father, Sir Tristram Lonsdale.

A very successful and wealthy artist, Sir Tristram had specialised in painting highly romantic scenes from medieval life, loosely based on ancient legends and fables. After inheriting a large private income, and being knighted by Queen Victoria—a great ad-mirer of his more gloomy paintings—Sir Tristram had begun travelling far and wide across the globe, returning from his many journeys with a re-markable assortment of weird and wonderful ob-jects. To these he had added a collection of ancient Greek and Roman remains, which his wife had inherited from her family, the original owners of the house.

Although Angelica wasn't too keen on some of the paintings, which she thought decidedly depressing, she deeply loved the eccentric house—and its even more eccentric contents. Because, as she frequently explained to visitors when the house was open to the public, the really marvellous thing about Sir Tristram's legacy was not only that he'd been an uncontrollable collector of just about everything under the sun, but that he had *never* allowed anything to be thrown away! As a consequence, the large house still contained not only a very valuable collection of Victorian paintings, but practically every room was full to overflowing with an extraordinary assortment of strange objects.

Realising that there ought to be a proper catalogue of all the various items—instead of the original, dusty labels written in Sir Tristram's spidery handwriting—Angelica had once attempted to compile a list of each room's contents. But after spending three weeks on the job, she had been dismayed to find that she'd barely scratched the surface—and had abandoned what seemed a hopeless task. Quite apart from trying to describe all the Greek and Roman statues, Peruvian pottery, Egyptian mummies, Chinese ceramics, rough gem stones and various objects in silver and gold, Angelica hadn't a clue where the collection of shrunken heads came from—Borneo, perhaps?— and she could only hazard a wild guess as to the use of some of those frightening, horrific-looking scientific instruments.

However, quite determined that his collection should be kept intact, Sir Tristram had formed a complicated trust—backed by a very large sum of money—to preserve the house and its contents for the interest of future generations. Unfortunately, almost one hundred years after his death, Sir Tristram Lonsdale's legacy was providing considerable difficulties for both his trustees and Angelica.

'Haven't you got that tea made yet?' Betty grumbled as she bustled into the kitchen. 'I don't know...a young girl like you, daydreaming all the time. What you need is a nice young man,' she added, sighing thankfully as she sank down into a comfortable chair.

'The *last* thing I want is a "nice young man", thank you very much! I haven't forgotten that rat, Nigel Browning, even if you have,' Angelica retorted grimly as she poured boiling water on to the tea-leaves in the pot.

'Yes, well...' Betty muttered, two high spots of colour flaring in her cheeks. 'I made a bit of a mistake there.'

'Let's face it, Betty—he charmed the socks off both of us,' Angelica sighed, reaching up into a cupboard for some cups and saucers.

How could she have been so foolish as to fall, hook, line and sinker, for that smooth-talking bastard Nigel Browning? Even now, almost a year later, Angelica simply couldn't understand why she'd been such an idiot. She'd had lots of casual boyfriends at university, of course. But her grandmother's long terminal illness had left her very little time for any private life. So maybe it was her youth and inexperience which had led to her becoming so blindly infatuated with the attractive rogue? Although even Betty—who was normally a very

shrewd judge of character—had also been capti-
vated by the rotten man's overwhelming charm.

Looking back at the distressing episode, she could
still feel almost sick with embarrassment. It was
humiliating to have to acknowledge what a fool
she'd made of herself—and over a man who was,
it transpired, nothing but a professional con man!
So professional, in fact, that it had taken Angelica
some time before she could bring herself to believe
the police, when they'd told her that Nigel had been
caught red-handed, trying to sell part of Sir
Tristram's valuable collection of gold snuff-boxes.

'That's the way it goes, sweetie. It was just my
bad luck to get caught,' he'd admitted with a shrug
and one of his charming smiles when she'd rushed
to the police station, quite convinced that he must
be the victim of a terrible mistake.

But it was clearly *she* who'd made such a terrible
mistake. Deeply scarred by the shame of having
been so easily duped, Angelica was determined that
she would never, *never* again allow herself to fall
so disastrously in love with anyone—let alone
Betty's idea of a 'nice young man'!

'Do you know what I need at the moment?' she
told the other woman as she poured them both a
cup of tea. 'What I *really* need is to get my hands
on a very large sum of money.'

Betty nodded. 'All that work on the roof isn't
going to come cheap. Do you reckon you've got
insurance cover for the storm damage?'

'I hope so,' Angelica sighed. 'But now that a
problem has also arisen over the roof timbers, I'm
just keeping my fingers crossed that the trust will
pay for the necessary repairs.' She gave an unhappy

shrug. 'If only we could find Mrs Eastman, maybe she and I could get together and really put this house in order.'

Following her grandmother's death over two years ago, Angelica had discovered that she was one of two heiresses to the property, sharing her inheritance with a very distant relative who apparently lived in America. Although the trustees had done their best to trace the woman—a Mrs Elizabeth Eastman, aged approximately sixty years of age, who was descended from a brother of old Sir Tristram—they had drawn a blank so far. However, until the other beneficiary had been found, the trustees had agreed that Angelica could continue to live in the house and receive a small income from the trust, providing that she maintain the house and open it once a week to interested visitors, as outlined in Sir Tristram's will.

None of which was a problem, Angelica told herself as she sipped the hot liquid. Having lived in the large old house with her grandmother, ever since her own parents' death in a car crash in France when she was only ten years old, she dearly loved the place which she'd always thought of as home. Unfortunately, keeping the old building in good repair seemed to take up virtually every penny of her income from the trust. Every day Lonsdale House seemed to become more and more expensive to maintain in good order. Although she'd managed to pay the bills so far, a large and worrying problem had arisen over the roof timbers, which were apparently in a terrible state and would have to be replaced.

How on earth was she going to find the money? The small amount of money she earned from working for David Webster wasn't enough to pay for her food, let alone anything else. And Betty had only a small private pension. It had seemed, therefore, that the obvious solution would be for her to try and get a full-time job. However, since open days at Lonsdale House required at least two people to be in attendance, that idea had proved to be totally impractical, because any salary she might earn would only have to go to pay the wages of a curator. It seemed to be an insuperable problem, and one which she couldn't seem to resolve however hard she tried.

'If only you could sell some of those paintings,' Betty said, echoing her own thoughts. 'There's one or two in the dining-room—nasty, gloomy things they are too!—which we could well do without.'

'It's no good.' Angelica shook her head. 'I've already tried to persuade the trustees to part with some of the minor paintings, which would certainly solve all our problems. But they simply won't budge from the terms of old Sir Tristram's will.'

'Well, I'd better get back to work before my old bones completely seize up,' Betty said, putting down her cup and easing herself up from the chair. 'And you'd better get a move on. I hope you're not intending to go out in those dirty old jeans?'

'No, of course not.' Angelica grinned, putting an affectionate arm around the elderly woman's stout figure as they left the kitchen. 'You know what your trouble is, don't you? You simply can't seem to understand that now I'm grown-up I no longer need a nanny!'

'Humph!'

'Anyway,' she continued, ignoring Betty's loud snort of derision, 'I've still got a lot of work to do before deciding what to wear for the tour this afternoon.'

'You'll have trouble finding anything decent,' Betty reminded her gloomily. 'With the rainwater gushing through that wardrobe of yours, it will be some time before we can get anything dried out.'

Angelica shrugged. 'Never mind—I expect I'll find something to wear. And as a last resort I can always raid Granny's old costume hampers. After all, it's only a short two-hour walk around the City. And since the group is likely to consist mostly of young students, it really won't matter *what* I look like,' she added as they continued to climb up the old oak staircase.

Later that afternoon, over four miles away in the City of London, Luke Cunningham had just finished signing the papers in front of him.

'OK, that's it, Norma.' He raised his head to give his middle-aged personal assistant a warm smile of approval. 'Is there anything else I ought to look at?'

'There is just one item. Mr Richards was anxious for you to see this, as soon as possible.' She handed him a file.

Gazing down at her boss, who was swiftly scanning the papers in front of him, Norma reflected that the last two years seemed to have passed by in a flash. Ever since the dynamic, high-powered Mr Cunningham had won the fierce take-over battle for Cornhill International, merging it with his own private merchant bank, it had seemed as if the whole of this huge, seven-storey office block in the City of London had been turned upside-down!

Almost from the first day he'd arrived in the office, news of Luke Cunningham's rapid expansion of the company had seldom been out of the financial press. With the newspapers full of stories about the 'Hot-Shot City Financier of the Nineties', Norma had been unsure about her ability to cope with such an energetic and vigorous man— who reportedly ate secretaries for breakfast! However, Mr Cunningham had seemed to be very pleased with her efforts. Quickly finding herself promoted to the post of his personal assistant, she'd also been given a massive rise in salary, and two extra girls to help share the workload in the office.

Despite being permanently run off her feet, she loved her job—even if her elderly, invalid mother was apt to become tetchy when Norma had to work late at the office. She also had the considerable satisfaction of knowing that she was deeply envied by almost every other woman in the building.

'I'd *kill* for your job—Mr Cunningham is *so* gorgeous and sexy!' one of the young typists had sighed the other day, before Norma had briskly put the silly girl firmly in her place.

However, as her eyes now flicked over his dark head, Norma couldn't help recalling a phrase often used in her favourite romantic novels. 'Tall, dark and handsome' was a description which might have been coined for the new chairman. Not only was he much taller than most men, there was something powerful and decidedly dangerous about the way he moved. Beneath the exquisitely cut, hand-tailored suit his body was lean and hard, with broad, muscular shoulders and narrow hips. His thick, dark hair swept down over his well-shaped head, clinging seductively to the nape of his neck, while his hard, tanned features and firm chin were those of a man to be reckoned with. It was an impression reinforced by the glittering grey eyes set beneath heavy eyelids, which even her middle-aged heart found profoundly disturbing.

And so did a lot of other women, Norma acknowledged wryly. A single multimillionaire of thirty-six, living in a small penthouse apartment overlooking Hyde Park, was bound to have a full social life. And Mr Cunningham was clearly no exception. Every day there seemed to be one glamorous female after another on the telephone—while his astronomically large bills for bouquets of flowers must surely be keeping the local florist in business!

Luke closed the file, leaning back in his leather chair for a moment, gazing at the shafts of brilliant sunlight streaming in through the large plate-glass window at the far end of the room.

'OK, Norma—tell Richards I'll see him tomorrow morning,' he said, before rising to his feet and walking slowly across the thick beige carpet.

Staring down through the window at the tall trees in a nearby churchyard, whose fresh green leaves were dancing in the light breeze, Luke was suddenly swept by an almost overwhelming urge to quit this modern, multi-storey building of glass and steel. And why not? It was far too nice a day to be cooped up inside a stuffy office block.

Ten minutes later, Luke had left the large building. Relishing the rare opportunity to stretch his legs and enjoy the bright sunshine of a warm June afternoon, he walked slowly down Bishopsgate, one of the main thoroughfares of the busy City of London.

Always fascinated by the history and ancient customs of the city in which he worked, he decided to stroll in the direction of the Thames, from whose docks and wharfs had flowed the wealth responsible for making London the heart of a world-wide trading empire. Striding through Leadenhall market with its ornate, glass-roofed arcade and on past the Monument, he crossed over London Bridge.

But when, some time later, he was slowly retracing his steps over the dark waters of the Thames, the sight of a young couple walking hand in hand reminded him it really was about time he came to a firm decision about Eleanor.

The senior partner of a prestigious accountancy firm, Eleanor Nicholson was a clever, forceful and sophisticated woman who'd made no secret of the fact that she wished to marry him. And he was quite sure that Eleanor would make a perfect wife. She was cool, calm and collected, and there was very little that was capable of disturbing her unruffled composure. She was always beautifully dressed, cooked like a dream and was a marvellous hostess. As one of his oldest male friends had pointed out the other day, what more could he possibly want?

He certainly wasn't looking for 'true love', Luke told himself with a wry, sardonic grin. Both he and Eleanor were in complete agreement on that score, neither of them having any time for such an untidy,

juvenile emotion. It had been very different when
he was younger, of course. Looking back at his
callow youth, it seemed to Luke as if he'd been violently infatuated with one totally unsuitable
woman after another! But now that he'd reached
a reasonably sober age in life—without ever having
permanently lost his head or his heart to any
woman—it was clearly time that he settled down to
a life of quiet, calm domesticity. And, since he was
taking Eleanor out to dinner at Le Gavroche
tomorrow night, that was obviously the ideal time
and place for a proposal of marriage.

Pleased to have come to a firm decision regarding his future, Luke's attention was drawn to
an odd assortment of people standing around the
base of the Monument. They appeared to be
listening to an extraordinary-looking girl, who was
pointing at the tall column behind her.

Despite telling himself that she was undoubtedly
a crazy, left-wing rabble-rouser, Luke was intrigued by the way the girl was dressed—and the
sight of her long and straight ash-blonde hair,
shimmering and sparkling in the bright sunlight. A
moment later, he found himself stepping off the
pavement and walking slowly across the road.

'And now we come to a very important point in
the history of the city of London—the Great Fire
of 1666,' Angelica told the group standing in front
of her.

Considering that she'd never done this particular
tour before, she was pleased at just how well things
had been going over the past half-hour. In fact,
although she was carrying a clipboard, holding a

map of the route and a few hastily scribbled notes, she'd hardly had to use it.

Of course, she was less than thrilled at having to wear these awful clothes, but they were the only garments she'd been able to find which hadn't been soaked by last night's rainstorm. Luckily, none of her group seemed at all perturbed by the weird ensemble of tight black and white striped leggings, topped by a gentleman's crimson silk waistcoat over a fine white lawn shirt edged with heavy lace ruffles at her neck and wrists. So who cared if she looked like the principal boy in a pantomime? All that mattered was the fact that, despite the narrow city streets which made it difficult to keep track of the numbers in her party, everyone still seemed to be with her—and really interested in what she had to say.

Proceeding to tell her audience of young backpacking Australians, some bored housewifes, two inscrutable Japanese businessmen and several elderly American tourists all about the Great Fire which had destroyed over eighty per cent of London, Angelica found that even she herself was becoming caught up in the drama of the story.

'The fire raged through the city for four days and nights, devastating over thirteen thousand houses and businesses, before it was finally put out. This column is known as the Monument.' She turned to put her hand on the tall stone edifice behind her. 'It was erected to commemorate the Great Fire, and——'

'No, I'm afraid that's not right.'

The sound of the deep voice, cutting across her flow of words, threw her into momentary confusion.

'Um—er——' She blinked, her wide blue eyes quickly scanning the group. However, since no one seemed disposed to say anything further, she decided to press on. 'As I was saying, this column was built to commemorate the Great Fire of 1666, and——'

'No! That piece of information is definitely *not* correct.'

The disembodied voice sounded much louder this time, causing her audience to swivel around to face a tall man standing at the back of the group.

'Now, just a minute!' she said sharply. It wasn't the first time some clever Dick had tried to disrupt a tour, and she knew that it was fatal to allow them to get away with it.

'I can assure you that the information I've just given you is quite correct,' she informed the group firmly. 'There *was* a Great Fire. It *did* destroy much of London. And this column commemorates that fact.'

'I hope our charming guide will forgive me for correcting her...?' the man drawled, raising a quizzical dark eyebrow as he walked slowly through the group towards her. 'However, I've always understood that the Monument was erected to commemorate the *rebuilding* of the city—not the fire itself.'

'That is nothing but a mere technicality,' Angelica muttered, her face flaming with embarrassment as she realised that the irritating man was quite right.

All the same...she was sure that this man, whose deep voice was tinged with a faint American accent, hadn't been with them from the start of the tour. Surely she wouldn't have overlooked such a tall and obviously commanding figure? And what was he doing on a tour like this, anyway? Now that he was standing only a few feet away, it was obvious that from the top of his handsome dark head, right down to those expensive, hand-made shoes, he clearly belonged to a world of wealth and privilege. In fact, clothed in that deathly smart, dark city suit, he stood out from the other members of the tour like a sleek raven amid a crowd of dusty sparrows.

It was, of course, an occupational hazard of the business that the tours, passing through crowded streets, were apt to attract the attention of passers-by. And if the guides didn't keep their wits about them, people would often take part without paying a fee.

Unfortunately she'd been so tired from having been up all night—and so nervous about following an unfamiliar route—that Angelica couldn't remember whether or not this man had been on their tour from the beginning.

Just as she was about to challenge his right to join them, Angelica was diverted by one of the Australian students. Noticing a door at the base of the Monument, he wondered if it were possible to climb up to the top.

'Yes, it is,' she told him. 'Unfortunately, we can't spare the time to do so today,' she added quickly.

'Oh, well, I guess I'll have to come back some other time and have a go. By the way, how many steps are there?'

Angelica stared at him, her mind a complete blank. The only thing was to make a guess at the number and hope for the best. 'Well—um——'

'There are three hundred and eleven steps,' a deep voice replied from just behind her shoulder, causing her to spin around to discover that the tall man was now standing just beside her.

'But it's a very tight spiral staircase—with definitely no room for a backpack!' he told the young Aussie with a grin. 'So if you want a good bird's-eye view of London, I'd recommend the Stone Gallery in St Paul's Cathedral.'

'Thanks, mate.'

'Do you mind?' she snapped at the tall stranger. '*I'm* the one who is supposed to be leading the tour!'

'Oh, really?' he drawled sardonically, his eyes gleaming with amusement. 'Then why haven't you mentioned the name of the architect who designed this column?'

'I was just getting around to that!' She scowled up at him. 'It was Sir Christopher Wren, of course.'

'Well done!' he murmured sarcastically. 'And now maybe you can tell us the height of the Monument?'

Angelica gritted her teeth. Why on earth would anyone want to know that piece of completely *useless* information?

'No, as it happens, I'm afraid that I can't quite—um—can't quite recall the exact figure...' she muttered, her face flaming as he gave a low, cynical laugh.

'Oh, dear!' he drawled, before turning towards the other members of the group. 'It would seem that our guide is suffering from temporary amnesia. She appears to have forgotten that the column is two hundred and two feet high.'

'Goodness me—isn't that interesting?' she exclaimed, determined to stop this man in his tracks, before he became any more of a flaming nuisance than he was already. 'I'm sure that we're all very grateful for that really *fascinating* piece of information,' she added grimly. 'And now I think we'd better get on with our tour, so...'

'But you haven't yet told us exactly *why* the column was built to that precise measurement.'

Simmering with fury, Angelica was swept by an almost overwhelming urge to slap that patronising, supercilious smile off the rotten man's handsome face. In fact, it was only the group of people—all clearly waiting for an answer—which prevented her from doing so.

'OK—you win. I'll admit that I don't know the answer,' she hissed through clenched teeth. 'But, since you obviously think you're so smart, why don't *you* tell everyone? In fact,' she yelled, suddenly losing her temper as his grin widened, 'why don't you take over this entire tour? I'm *sure* that you think you can do a better job than I can. Right?'

'I certainly couldn't do any worse!' he agreed with a bark of cynical laughter. 'However, the answer is that it's exactly two hundred and two feet from this spot to where the fire originally started, in the baker's shop in Pudding Lane.'

'Oh, wow—big deal!' she ground out. 'So—who cares, anyway?'

'Aw, come on, honey...!' An elderly American woman patted the girl's arm. 'We all reckon you're doing a good job. But you've got to admit that those sort of facts are kinda interesting.'

'Yes, well, I suppose so...' Angelica sighed before taking a deep breath and trying to simmer down.

Determinedly ignoring the tall, dark stranger, she gathered the other members of the party together, warning them that they must hurry since the tour was now running behind schedule. However, as she led the group down Lower Thames Street towards the Tower of London, she couldn't help wishing that they could be transported back to Tudor times.

What wouldn't she give to see that truly *awful* man kneeling at the block on Tower Green—and an executioner with a deadly sharp axe standing by, ready to chop off his handsome head!

CHAPTER TWO

By the time she was nearing the end of the walk, and approaching St Helen's Church in Bishopsgate, Angelica was almost foaming at the mouth with overwhelming rage and fury.

There was absolutely no doubt in her mind. She knew—with total certainty—that she'd *never* hated anyone as much as she did this truly awful man, who'd somehow managed to hijack her tour.

Every time she'd pointed out some interesting facts about the streets and buildings they'd passed, he had either flatly contradicted her small store of knowledge, or he'd produced some far more entertaining or unusual information. When she, for instance, had taken them into Trinity Square Gardens, to view the Merchant Navy memorial to the ships and men lost in the two World Wars, the group had barely listened to what she had to say. They'd been far more interested in hearing from Mr Know-it-all that they were standing on the official site of bloody public executions, which had been carried out there until the seventeenth century.

Nor had the group cared a jot about Seething Lane, which had once held the Navy Office in which the famous diarist Samuel Pepys had worked, not when the dreadful man had loudly complained that the tour was boring, before leading everyone across the road to St Olave's church. And then, adding insult to injury, the group had completely ignored

her as he'd not only showed them around the
churchyard where Pepys and his wife were buried,
but also told them that the gateway of this church—
with its macabre decoration of skulls—had fea-
tured in one of Charles Dickens's famous novels.

And so it had gone on. At practically every step
along their route, the tall stranger had succeeded
in making her look like a complete idiot. Goodness
knew, that was bad enough—but what made it ten
times worse was that he'd clearly been enjoying
every minute of her discomfiture! He also seemed
to have taken a delight in asking her questions which
he knew that she couldn't answer. Quite honestly,
she could quite cheerfully have throttled the man!

As she waited for the stragglers of the group to
join the others inside St Helen's church, which
dated back to at least the twelfth century, Angelica
knew that she must try to do something about the
situation. But what?

Cudgelling her brains to try and think of some
way in which to regain control of the final part of
the tour, Angelica noticed that the loathsome man
had moved away from the group, and was apparently absorbed in studying a beautifully carved
Jacobean pulpit. Quickly realising that she might
not have another opportunity to catch him on his
own, she moved swiftly down one of the two wide
aisles towards his tall figure.

'Hey—I want a word with you, sunshine!' she
hissed, tapping him sharply on the shoulder, before
leading the way around the side of the pulpit to a
dark corner well out of sight of the group. Spinning
around, she waited impatiently as he hesitated for
a moment before moving slowly towards her.

'I don't know what you think you've been doing, you damned man!' she ground out through clenched teeth. 'But it's going to stop—right now!'

For a moment he stared at her in complete astonishment, as if stunned that anyone could have the sheer effrontery to swear at him in public. Well, if so, that was just his tough luck! Because, by the time *she'd* finished with this man, Angelica promised herself grimly, he was going to be well and truly cut down to size!

'Well, Miss...?' He paused, but when she kept her mouth firmly closed he gave a casual shrug of his broad shoulders. 'I'm not quite sure what you're talking about.'

'Oh, yes, you are! As far as I'm concerned, you've been nothing but a rotten pain in the neck ever since you joined this group.'

'Really?'

'Yes—*really*!' she snapped, infuriated by the note of sardonic amusement in his deep voice.

Despite the lack of clear daylight within the large old church, Angelica had no trouble in seeing that, having swiftly recovered from her first attack, the man's grey eyes were now gleaming with ironic laughter beneath their heavy lids. A fact which only served to increase her rage and fury.

'Don't you dare laugh at me!' she spat through gritted teeth. 'Because, to start with, I *know* that you didn't pay to join this walking tour.'

'Didn't I?' he murmured, leaning casually against the wooden pulpit, his lips twitching with amusement as he surveyed the furiously angry, trembling figure of the girl before him.

'No, you damn well didn't!'

'Tut, tut!' He shook his dark head in mock-sorrow. 'I'm shocked to hear a young girl swearing like this—and in church, too.'

For the first and only time in her life, Angelica had an almost overpowering urge to resort to real physical violence, a deep longing to vigorously slap that cynical, amused expression off the man's handsome face. However, after a fierce internal struggle, she took a deep breath and managed to pull herself together.

'OK...let me explain the situation in words of one syllable,' she ground out. 'If you haven't paid to join this tour, you've got no right to be here with us.'

'Well, I don't know about that...' he drawled slowly. 'You clearly have very little knowledge about the City of London. In fact, since I've been doing your job for the past half-hour, maybe *you* should pay me, hmm?' he murmured, moving closer to the rigidly angry figure.

'Me? *Pay you*...?' She gave a strangled, in-credulous laugh. 'Don't be ridiculous!'

'It's no more ridiculous than taking money under false pretences—which is exactly what you've been doing,' he pointed out coolly. 'If I hadn't come along to rescue you, this tour would have been a complete shambles.'

'Rubbish!' Angelica retorted defiantly, raising her chin and refusing to be intimidated by the tall, handsome figure looming over her in the dark corner of the church. 'I may not be a walking en-cyclopaedia, but I was getting along fine until *you* turned up.'

'Now who's talking rubbish?' He gave a low, mocking laugh. 'In fact, I'm not sure it isn't my duty—as a moral and upright citizen—to report you to the authorities.'

'I don't care *what* you do!' she stormed. 'Just as long as you get out of my hair, out of this church, and that I never, *ever* have to see you again!'

Quite why she thought that she was strong enough to push the handsome, dark stranger away from her, and out of the church, Angelica had no idea. But of course there was no rational thought process behind her total loss of temper.

It was only when the fiery red mist in front of her eyes had begun to clear that she realised her hands were being gripped by firm, hard fingers, tightening about her wrists like bands of steel. Prevented from hitting the awful man, she instinctively resorted to the use of her feet. But, although he gave a slight grunt of pain when her shoe connected with his shin, he didn't allow her to inflict any more damage. A brief moment or two later, Angelica found herself being pushed roughly backwards; the man's angry, determined momentum only halted as she felt her spine jar against cold stone, with his tall figure pinning her to a buttress in a dark corner of the church.

Shocked and severely shaken by the speed with which he'd reacted to her assault, she gazed fearfully up at the man glaring down at her, his face only inches away from her own. Despite the dim light, she was able to see a pulse beating furiously at his temple, the tightly clenched jaw and glittering, cold gleam in his deeply hooded grey eyes.

'Let me go!' she gasped helplessly. 'You can't do this to me!'

'No? Well, it seems that I can—and I have!' he growled savagely.

Badly frightened by the situation in which she now found herself—which was solely due, she realised with a sinking heart, to her own totally foolish loss of temper—Angelica desperately tried to free herself from the man's fierce grip.

'Let—me—go!' she panted, frantically redoubling her efforts to escape, and wincing with pain as his iron-like fingers tightened about her wrists.

'I've had quite enough of this nonsense,' he told her softly, the silky ruthlessness in his voice sending a shudder of fright through her trembling figure. 'I have every intention of letting you go. But *not* until you've calmed down,' he added, the dark anger in his face slowly subsiding as he gazed down at the struggling girl with an expression of guarded amusement.

'You...you can't keep me here!' she lashed back angrily, almost weeping with frustration, and an overpowering sense of her own folly in attempting to confront this apparently invincible man. 'If you don't let me go, I'll call the police! I'll scream and——'

'Oh, no, you won't!' he retorted, responding to her wild threats by swiftly raising his arm, whose wrist bore a wafer-thin gold watch, and placing a large, tanned hand over her mouth.

'I don't know what you think you're doing,' he added grimly over her muffled protests, 'but I'm not prepared to have my picture on the front page

of the gutter press. Nor to have my career in the
City ruined by some crazy, hysterical girl!'

Totally confused by the swift turn of events,
Angelica glared up at the man looming over her.
Effectively prevented from saying anything by the
large, warm hand firmly clamped over her trembling lips, she could do nothing to combat his height
and superior strength, which was keeping her im-
mobile and silent until he chose to let her go. And
where were the rest of the group? Why hadn't
someone come to her rescue? she wondered, her
eyes desperately probing the darkness behind the
man's tall, menacing figure.

'Are you going to be sensible?' he drawled
quietly, gazing down at the girl's flushed cheeks,
her wide blue eyes brimming with unshed tears of
acute frustration. 'There's no reason why we can't
discuss any problems you might have like two perfectly calm, responsible adults. So, if I take my hand
away, will you promise not to scream the place
down?' he added, waiting until she gave a reluctant
nod before slowly lowering his arm.

With hindsight, Angelica might have been prepared to admit that maybe the man wasn't *entirely*
to blame for what happened next. It was, after all,
just possible that he misunderstood the loud gasp
of relief which she gave on the removal of his hand.
But as she opened her mouth to take a deep gulp
of air, he appeared to assume that she was about
to break her promise.

As he ground out, 'Oh, no, you *don't*!' she found
herself crushed tightly to his chest, the fingers of
one hand burying themselves in her blonde hair,
holding her head firmly against him. She barely had

time to register the grim warning in his glittering grey eyes before he swiftly lowered his dark head towards her, preventing her from saying or doing anything as his mouth closed firmly over her lips.

It was a savage, ruthless kiss, clearly intended to stifle any sound or cry for help. Attempting to move her head or to escape proved useless. Becoming almost faint beneath the force of his lips and her own exertion, she drummed her fists against his broad shoulders in a vain and hopeless attempt to free herself from his tight embrace.

The next few minutes seemed somehow blurred in her mind. Shocked and totally disoriented by the speed with which she'd been assaulted, Angelica only dimly realised that the mouth which had so firmly possessed her own was no longer burning like a firebrand on her lips. Dazed and confused, she fluttered her eyelids open, to see him gazing down at her with a tense, strained expression on his hard features. The hands which had been gripping her so fiercely were now gently holding her face as his fingers moving softly over the contours of her pale cheeks.

'I don't know what the hell's going on. I must be out of my mind!' he breathed huskily as she continued to stare blindly up at him, her dazed brain unable to comprehend what was happening to her.

It seemed as though she was viewing the scene from afar—almost as if it was happening to someone else—her senses beguiled by the musky scent of his cologne, and the hard strength of the body pressed closely to her own. Her whole world seemed encompassed by the darkening glitter in the grey eyes, now staring down at her so intently.

Since she was mentally paralysed, there seemed nothing she could do as he lowered his head to brush his lips softly over her mouth. By the time she had begun to comprehend the almost impossible fact that he was intending to kiss her—*yet again*!—it was far too late for any effective protest.

As if in a dream, she became slowly aware of an insidious rising tide of sensual excitement, which flowed like molten lava through every part of her body, the wild beating of her heart echoing like a drum in her ears, her lips parting helplessly beneath the deepening force of his kiss. And then she was lost, responding blindly and with an increasing urgency to the taut, male body pressed so firmly to her softly yielding breasts and thighs.

Suddenly it was all over as she found herself abruptly released. Swiftly pushing her away, he took a step backwards, cursing harshly beneath his breath and brushing a hand roughly through his thick, dark hair.

Dazed and trembling, Angelica stared at him in complete confusion, her gaze only slowly following his as he turned to look behind him. What she saw then was enough to make her almost faint with embarrassment and deep mortification. Because not only had the tour group finally tracked her down, but, from the look of astonishment on some faces and the wide grins on others, it was obvious that they had been interested observers of all that had just taken place!

*   *   *

Many hours later, as she lay in the comforting darkness of her own bedroom at Lonsdale House, Angelica could still feel herself going hot and cold with shame at the recollection of the humiliating scene. At the time, she simply hadn't been able to cope with the acutely distressing episode, firmly closing her eyes for some moments and desperately trying to think what she could possibly say or do next. The realisation that she had no option but to continue with the tour had been almost more than she could bear. And yet, when she'd finally forced herself to open her eyes, she'd discovered that the group—possibly to save her any further embarrassment and chagrin—had melted away. And so, too, had the tall stranger.

In fact, although she'd somehow managed to re-assemble her group of walkers, giving no one the chance of discussing what they'd seen as she led them swiftly through the remainder of the tour, she luckily hadn't set eyes on the awful man again. It was almost as though he'd vanished into thin air. He'd certainly left the church before she did. And although Angelica had thrown cautious glances up and down the street, before turning right to cross the piazza towards the church of St Andrew Undershaft and on down Leadenhall Street, he'd been nowhere to be seen.

It would have been a comfort if she could have dismissed the scene from her mind, as if it had all been a bad dream or nightmare. Unfortunately, it was impossible to pretend that it had been a figment of her overheated imagination. Especially when she could all too easily recall the effect of his kiss on her emotions, the tide of sick excitement flooding through her body as she once more relived the feel of the hard, firm lips and body pressed so closely to her own.

With a groan, she turned over to bury her face in the pillow. She must . . . she simply *must* try and forget the whole hideous incident. It was stupid to be reacting in such a childish way to a confrontation which, if she was to be truly honest, had been partly her own fault. If she hadn't so spectacularly lost her temper, the shameful episode would never have happened. Her only sensible course of action, therefore, must now be to try and dismiss the whole affair from her mind.

After all, she knew nothing about the man or where he came from—not even his name. Fortunately, there was no possibility of his knowing anything about her either. Since she'd never guided a walking tour of the City before—and she certainly wouldn't ever attempt to do so again!—the odds on their ever meeting in the future must be about a million to one. It was a comforting thought that brought a measure of peace to her troubled mind, and one which enabled her at last to drift slowly off into a dreamless sleep.

The next few days seemed to pass by in a whirl. Angelica was kept so busy trying to sort out the deeply depressing problems concerning the roof timbers, and worrying about how to find the money to pay for the essential repairs, that she barely had time to think about her disastrous encounter with the strange man.

She wasn't just concerned with problems about the roof, of course. Not only had it been a mammoth exercise to take most of her clothes to the dry-cleaners, but she'd also been forced to call in professional firms both to dry the large Persian carpets and to inspect the valuable paintings—all yet more unavoidable expense.

It didn't seem to matter how many times she did her sums, the figures obstinately refused to add up. From the way the money was flowing out of her account, it wouldn't be long before she found herself in serious financial trouble. In fact, after receiving two tough warning letters from her bank manager, it looked as if she was going to have to take some drastic action very soon.

Luckily there had been no fall-out from her tour of the City. Not wishing to look for trouble, she'd been very careful and guarded when talking on the phone to her boss, David Webster. Knowing just how pessimistic he could be, she was certain that he'd have informed her immediately of any complaints or comments about her proficiency as a guide. So it seemed as though the tall, unknown man was every bit as anxious as she was to forget the whole distasteful incident.

It was, therefore, with a reasonably light heart that she prepared to set out, a few afternoons later, on her next tour of London.

Entitled *The Village of Chelsea*, it explored the highways and byways of what had once been a small village, surrounded by country estates and summer palaces belonging to royalty, and some of the most interesting men and women in the history of British art and literature.

It was a tour which she had personally designed and put together, taking place on the same day every week as laid down in the small printed brochures produced by David. With Lonsdale House situated in Cheyne Walk, overlooking the River Thames, the tour also had the great merit of taking place virtually outside her own front door. Besides which, guiding people around her favourite area of London for a leisurely, two-hour stroll in the warm sunshine, was nothing but a pleasure and a delight. And, since there was no possibility of being faced by the nervous apprehension which had overtaken her in the City a few days ago, Angelica was feeling happily confident as she ran downstairs into the large hall.

'That's a definite improvement,' Betty said, eyeing the girl's fresh summer dress, whose plain fitted bodice and softly gathered skirt emphasised her slim waist. Angelica had pinned her long, pale gold hair into a loose knot on top of her head, small tendrils of hair escaping to frame her face with soft curls, her wide blue eyes reflecting the colour of her blue cotton dress.

'I don't know *what* you think you looked like the other day. It was a disgraceful sight, and I can only hope that you didn't meet anyone we know,' the older woman added grimly, before continuing her job of dusting the marble busts of long-dead Roman emperors, set on plinths in the hall.

'Don't be such an old fuss-pot!' Angelica grinned. 'You know very well that, with everything sopping wet, the only thing I could do was to raid Granny's boxes of theatrical costumes.'

'Yes, I suppose so.' Betty gave a heavy sigh. 'I still miss your grandma so much, you know. Not a day goes by when I don't think of all the fun times we used to have together in the theatre.'

'Yes, I know,' Angelica murmured sympathetically.

She, too, deeply regretted the loss of her grandmother. Even in her old age and during her last, long illness, the elderly woman had possessed a bright, sparkling mind and a vibrant personality. Angelica knew, from the trunks of old costumes, photographs and posters, that her grandmother had once been outstandingly beautiful, and a star on the musical comedy stage, before leaving the bright lights behind her to marry old Sir Tristram's grandson. Betty, who'd been her dresser in the theatre for many years, had insisted on accompanying her to Lonsdale House where, as her old nanny had so often pointed out, they'd all lived happily every after.

'Ooo...the parties we used to have!' Betty murmured, pausing in her dusting to stare into space for a moment. 'There always seemed to be so much life and laughter in this house. But nowadays it's more like a morgue,' she added with a heavy sigh.

Angelica had to admit that Betty was right. She herself could just remember the glittering dinner parties and crowded, exciting receptions which had taken place when she'd been a small girl. However, as her grandmother had grown older and more infirm, fewer and fewer people had come to the house. Following her grandmother's death two years ago, the large building now seemed to have become nothing but a dusty museum. Although Angelica made sure that Lonsdale House was open to the public once a week—as she was obliged to do by the terms of the trust—they very seldom had more than one or two visitors.

She really couldn't blame people for not coming to the house in droves, she told herself glumly. Sir Tristram's collection might be an interesting and fascinating one, but even she could see that the whole place required a completely radical overhaul. But, in order to put a fresh approach into action, she knew that she would need both expert advice and a great deal of money.

'You'd better hurry up. If you don't get a move on, you'll be late!' Betty's warning voice broke into her dismal thoughts.

'Yes—you're right,' Angelica muttered with a quick glance at one of the many large clocks scattered about the hall. Swiftly gathering up her handbag, she ran towards the front door. 'Oh, by the way, I won't be back until quite late this afternoon,' she added. 'I've promised to go and have tea with old Lady Marshall.'

'Rather you than me, any day. That old hag is a right battleaxe!' the older woman called out, her scornful peal of laughter echoing in Angelica's ears as she hurried down the street.

There was clearly no love lost between her old nanny and Lady Marshall. Unfortunately, Betty had known the imperious old lady when she'd been plain Doreen Summers, kicking up her legs in the back row of the chorus. 'A very flighty piece she was, too,' Betty had said. 'If Doreen hadn't caught old Sir Edward Marshall's eye, and frogmarched him to the altar, goodness *knows* where she might have ended up!'

However, as Angelica got off the bus at Sloane Square, she was far less interested in Lady Marshall's past than in her present position as chairman of the board of trustees responsible for the maintenance and upkeep of Lonsdale House. Of course, Betty was quite right. There was no doubt that the elderly lady was an extremely tiresome and difficult woman. Unfortunately, with her very strong, forceful personality, she had become the dominant voice among the other trustees, who all weakly bowed to her will.

Having greeted the group of people gathered together for her tour, with some latecomers still arriving, Angelica was still preoccupied with wondering exactly how to deal with Lady Marshall. It was vitally important that the elderly woman should fully understand the immediate, desperate problems she was now facing with Lonsdale House.

Collecting the small fee for the tour, and automatically handing back the small yellow receipts, plus any necessary change, Angelica was just wondering if she could put forward the idea of obtaining advice from the Victoria and Albert Museum, when a deeply voiced 'thank you' caught her attention.

Looking more closely at the long, tanned fingers of the hand into which she was just placing a receipt, whose wrist was clasped by a distinctly familiar, wafer-thin gold watch, she suddenly felt faint. All the breath seemed to have been driven from her body, as though she'd been hit by a swift, violent blow to the solar plexus. Feeling quite sick, her eyes slowly travelled up the dark sleeve of the immaculately cut suit towards the broad shoulders and . . .

This couldn't be happening to her! Angelica clamped her eyelids tightly shut for a moment, fervently praying that she was mistaken. Could she be suffering from a very brief, temporary hallucination? But when she opened her dazed blue eyes again she realised that she was way out of luck. Because standing there and regarding her with a mocking, sardonic smile was the man who'd caused her such distress and emotional trauma only a few days ago.

'What are *you* doing here?' she gasped breathlessly.

'I thought it might be interesting to learn something about the history of Chelsea,' he drawled coolly, his lips twitching with amusement at her expression of consternation and horror. 'I'm also looking forward to seeing if you are any better informed about this area of London than you were about the City.'

Ignoring the hateful man's slur on her competence, Angelica quickly tried to pull herself together. 'Go away!' she spat through clenched teeth. 'I don't want to have anything to do with you!'

'Well, I'm afraid that you don't have any choice in the matter,' he murmured sardonically, holding up the yellow receipt. 'You have taken my money—which means that we now have a contract between us.'

What was it about this terrible man which could send her into a blind fury in just five seconds flat? Angelica asked herself wrathfully. And did paying his money *really* give him a lawful right to join the tour?

'So, OK—go ahead and sue me!' she ground out defiantly. 'Because you are definitely, absolutely *not* accompanying me on this tour today.'

The man raised a dark eyebrow, staring down at her blandly for a moment, before reaching inside his expensive dark suit. Producing an equally expensive-looking leather wallet, he extracted a small white business card.

'My dear girl, I have no intention of suing *you*,' he informed her coolly. 'However, if you continue to refuse to allow me to join this tour, I suggest that you give my card to your employer. You can tell him that he'll be hearing from my lawyers— about a possible action for damages.'

'A *what*...?' Angelica stared up at him in dawning horror. 'You've got to be kidding?'

The man shook his dark head. 'By using totally incompetent guides such as yourself, your employer is clearly responsible for taking money under false pretences,' he drawled silkily. Placing his business card in her nervously shaking hand, he added, 'I can assure you that it will give me great pleasure—plus the considerable satisfaction of performing a public duty, of course—to put both him and his ramshackle firm out of business.'

'You...you can't possibly *do* that!' she protested angrily.

'Would you like to place a bet on it?' he drawled, the hard, confident note in his voice sending shivers of fright scudding up and down her spine.

He gazed past her, to where the other members of the group were clearly becoming restless.

'It would seem that you have only a few seconds to come to a decision, Angelica. If you delay any longer, it looks as though I'm not going to be the *only* client to complain about the way your employer runs his business!'

CHAPTER THREE

THIS was definitely *not* one of her better tours, Angelica told herself glumly, staring blindly at an oil painting on the wall, while the other members of her group inspected the ancient hammer-beam roof and oriel windows of Crosby Hall.

She'd had no choice but to give in, of course. Despite practically dancing with rage in the middle of Sloane Square, Angelica had quickly realised that the awful man's dire threats to sue her employer, David Webster, had virtually settled the argument. She wouldn't have minded standing up in the High Court and telling the whole world *just* how objectionable the man really was. In fact, she'd have relished the chance to do so! But she really couldn't expose poor David to the possibility of legal proceedings. Especially when the conflict had absolutely nothing to do with the conduct of his business, and far more—if she was to be entirely honest—with an overwhelming personality clash between herself and the man, whose name appeared to be Luke Cunningham.

'This doesn't mean a thing!' she'd snorted, grimacing at the small white business card which he'd placed in her hand. 'It wouldn't take you more than five minutes to have one of these printed—with any name you chose to put on it. For all I know, you could be Jack the Ripper!' she'd added belligerently, squinting down in the sunshine at the small print, which merely stated in capital letters 'LUKE CUNNINGHAM', and in the bottom left-hand corner the words 'Cornhill Bank, Bishopsgate'.

'Don't be so stupid—of course that's my real name!' he snapped, clearly annoyed and put out by her temerity in suggesting otherwise.

'Oh, yes?' she queried sarcastically, before giving a bark of jeering, scornful laughter which she hoped he would find profoundly irritating. Although Angelica was well aware, from the sounds of general unrest in the group behind her, that she couldn't afford to stand here arguing with this man for much longer, she was quite determined to fight Mr Luke Cunningham every inch of the way.

'If you think that I'm likely to be impressed by the fact that you work in a bank, you couldn't be more wrong!' she added scathingly. 'Bank managers are definitely *not* my favourite people at the moment.'

'Well, in that case you will be relieved to hear that I most certainly am *not* a bank manager!' he told her grimly, a stormy glint of anger in his hooded grey eyes.

'So, OK, you're a lowly worm, slaving away behind the till. So *who cares*?' she exclaimed, before deliberately tearing up his business card and tossing the bits high up into the air.

Almost laughing out loud at the expression of indignation and outrage on his handsome, tanned face as the little white pieces fluttered slowly down on to the pavement about his feet, Angelica nervously stood her ground as he took a threatening step forward.

'It's clearly time that someone gave you a good hiding!' he growled. 'And, believe me, I'd be happy to volunteer for the job!'

'I just bet you would, you . . . you pervert!'

'*What* did you say?'

'I can see it all now,' she ground out furiously, refusing to be intimidated by his tall, dominant figure, or the dark brows drawn together in a startled, angry frown. 'That explains why you assaulted me the other day, right? I might have known that you're the awful, disgusting sort of man who gets his kicks from attacking strange women. Well, you'd better not try it again, *sunshine*—not unless you want to be arrested and thrown into gaol! Because I must have at least twenty witnesses back there.' She gestured behind her towards the group of walkers impatiently waiting for the tour to begin.

Angrily defiant, she was both astounded and totally confused when he suddenly threw back his head, and roared with laughter.

'Oh, Angelica! What an amazingly funny girl you are!' he declared, his broad shoulders shaking with amusement. 'However, just before you clap me in prison,' he added with a mocking grin, 'I'd be fascinated to hear your explanation of just *why* you responded so enthusiastically to my—er—assault the other day?'

'I did no such thing!' she gasped, her face flaming with embarrassment as he gave a low, taunting laugh.

'Oh, yes, you most certainly did. And very enjoyable it was too!'

Speechless with indignation, she scowled up at him, frantically trying to think of a sufficiently deadly, devastating response which would put this poisonous man firmly in his place, once and for all.

Unfortunately, before Angelica managed to construct a suitably crushing reply, she was distracted by the approach of an elderly American gentleman.

'Excuse me, miss, but are we going on this walk or aren't we?' he enquired plaintively.

Not giving her time to say or do anything, Luke Cunningham—clearly an oily snake in the grass—quickly seized control of the situation.

'That is precisely what I've been trying to find out,' he told the other man smoothly. 'However, I believe that our charming young guide is now ready to lead us on our way. Right, Angelica . . . ?'

Even now, almost an hour later, she was still steaming with anger at the way she'd been so cleverly out-manoeuvred. And how on earth had he managed to discover her name?

It was a deeply worrying question, which had buzzed away in her mind as she'd led the group past Sir Christopher Wren's Royal Hospital. She was ashamed of barely giving them time to appreciate either the classical architecture, or the aged Chelsea pensioners in their long, cardinal-red coats and black hats as they strolled about the quadrangle, or sat on the benches enjoying the sun beating down on their old bones.

Despite being preoccupied with her own problems, and anxious to keep as far away from Luke Cunningham as possible, Angelica had been forced to keep a sharp eye on her group when they reached the King's Road. The crowded street was always very popular with anyone under the age of forty,

mainly for its renown as one of *the* places in the
Swinging Sixties, as well as its present-day repu-
tation for smart shops and trendy boutiques.
Luckily, today's trip had been fairly uneventful,
with her only once having forcibly to drag two
young students from a crowded, noisy record shop.

However, the group had been genuinely interested
in knowing that the King's Road had been named
after Charles II, who'd adopted the route as his
private carriageway.

'I know it isn't easy, trying to imagine what it
must once have been like,' she said, when some
members of the party were clearly finding it difficult to ignore the wide streets and pavements,
which were now thronged with people enjoying the
many shops, restaurants and antique markets.

'It was originally just a very quiet country lane,
which lay between the King's main palaces of St
James and Hampton Court,' she continued. 'And,
in order to preserve his privacy, it was only open
to courtiers and wealthy members of the public, on
production of a copper pass.'

All that was in the past, of course, she'd explained, although subsequent kings had jealously
preserved their private right of way, with George
III being especially fond of travelling along this
route to one of his favourite palaces, at Kew.

If she hadn't appeared to have lost her normally
good sense of humour, Angelica might have found
some grim amusement when she and the group had
eventually reached Crosby Hall, situated near the
Thames Embankment, at the furthermost point of
their circular tour.

The fifteenth century hall had once formed part of a very large city mansion, owned and lived in by many famous people, including Sir Thomas More, on whose rural country estate much of modern-day Chelsea had been built, and also Sir Walter Raleigh, who'd brought back from his voyages to America such items as the potato plant and tobacco.

When the Great Hall had survived a fire which completely destroyed the rest of the large building, it had been dismantled and moved to Chelsea from its original site in Bishopsgate.

She seemed doomed by that particular area of the City, Angelica told herself grimly, wondering if she would *ever* be able to forget the embarrassing tour—and trying very hard not to look in the direction of Luke's tall, dark figure as she imparted the information to the rest of the group.

They were now still only three-quarters of the way through the walk, and she honestly wasn't sure that she was going to be able to stay the course. Quite apart from the sheer nervous exhaustion of having to be desperately careful not to make any small, careless errors—and thus giving Luke Cunningham an opportunity once again to make her look an absolute idiot—it was also the dominant physical presence of the loathsome man which was causing her to feel so tense and jittery.

Actually, to be fair, Luke hadn't pointed out any mistakes, or generally made a nuisance of himself, as he'd done during that disastrous walk around the City a few days ago. Which brought her strait back to square one, she told herself gloomily. Because the only thing which had made her rec-

ollection of that horrendous episode at all bearable
had been the realisation that not only would she
never see him again, but also the comforting
thought that he had no way of being able to trace
her. However, the discovery that she'd apparently
been living in a fool's paradise was now causing a
host of awkward questions to flood her tired mind.

If Luke had, somehow, discovered her name, it
was just possible that he might—God forbid!—turn
up at Lonsdale House. The cringing embarrassment which would result from her having to explain, to either Betty or her friends, just how she'd
met the awful man—and exactly what had happened—was almost more than she could bear.

She didn't, of course, really believe that Luke
was some kind of pervert—an insult which she'd
only thrown at him in the heat of their furious argument. But she had no doubt that he was quite
capable of causing her the maximum amount of
trouble and embarrassment. Especially if he decided to retaliate by explaining—in graphic detail—
how she'd lost her temper, and the measures he'd
taken to prevent her from crying out for help. Even
just thinking about it was enough to cause cold
beads of perspiration to break out on her forehead.

'I'm sure that's an interesting picture, but I think
the other members of our group would like to get
on with this tour.'

Startled by the dreaded sound of his deep voice
breaking into her distracted thoughts, Angelica
spun around to find Luke standing close beside her.

'Go away...get lost!' she snapped nervously,
trying to edge away from his tall, broad-shouldered
figure. Although she'd managed, so far, to keep

well out of his way during the walk, she might have known that her luck had been too good to last.

'My dear girl—surely your job is to make sure that we *don't* get lost?' he queried smoothly, his lips twitching with amusement at the smouldering fury in her wide blue eyes.

'Ha, ha, very funny!' she ground out, wondering what she'd ever done to deserve being plagued and hounded by this awful man. 'So, what do you want?' she added belligerently.

He shrugged. 'I merely wanted to tell you that I'm finding this a very interesting tour.'

'Hey—wow! Be still, my beating heart!' she gasped, dramatically clasping her hands to her chest and rolling her eyes up at the ceiling for a moment, before lowering her head to throw him a glance of acute dislike.

'Actually, Mr Cunningham,' she continued as he grinned down at her, 'I was just wondering why you've been so silent. Especially since you're obviously a walking encyclopaedia on the history of London. Surely there must have been *something* I've missed? One or two interesting and little-known facts with which you can bore us all to tears?' she ground out acidly.

If she'd hoped to annoy this man seriously—and, of course, she had—Angelica found that she was doomed to disappointment as he gave an amused shake of his head.

'Oh, dear, I do seem to have got under your skin, don't I?' He smiled down at her, before glancing at his wristwatch. 'However, despite the fact that we seem to be running a bit late, I would say that you appear to have been doing really very well.'

'Don't you dare patronise me!' she hissed, resolutely steeling herself to ignore the powerful effect
of his warm smile. He might not be a thief, like
Nigel Browning, but Luke clearly seemed to believe
that he, too, could charm the birds from the trees.

It had been obvious from the start of this afternoon's walk that for some quite inexplicable reason
most of the female members of the group had
clearly been drawn to the odious man's handsome
face and figure. Despite keeping well out of his way,
Angelica still had two perfectly good eyes in her
head—and it was quite disgusting, the way that
flashy redhead, for instance, had been openly
flirting with him! Serve the brazen hussy right when
she finds out *just* how awful he can be, Angelica
told herself grimly, her palms itching to slap the
oh-so-charming smile off his handsome face.

He gave a heavily dramatic sigh. 'OK, I give up!'

'What?' She frowned up at him in puzzlement.

'I've been trying to figure out why such a
beautiful girl should, on the two brief occasions on
which I've seen her, prove to be so thoroughly bad-
tempered.'

'I can easily solve that little problem,' she flashed
back quickly. 'Just as soon as I find out how you
discovered my name?'

'Ah.' He grinned infuriatingly down at her.
'We—er—"lowly worms" in the banking world
have ways and means of ferreting out such
information.'

'I'm sure you have!' Angelica ground out in a
low voice as some members of the group passed
them on their way out of the hall. 'And if that expensive suit of yours is anything to go by, I expect

you've also had your sticky fingers in the bank's till!' she added spitefully, enraged by his refusal to answer her question.

But it seemed that he was impervious to provocation, as he merely responded with a deep rumble of laughter.

'Come on, you maddening girl,' he said, putting an arm about her waist as he led her towards the door, blandly ignoring the way she jumped like a nervous, startled cat at the touch of his hand on her body.

'If you don't get a move on, you'll be in danger of losing all the other members of the group,' he told her in a mocking drawl. 'And, although I can't imagine why, I have the distinct impression that you *really* wouldn't like to be left alone here with me!'

How right he was! Angelica told herself grimly, hurrying along the road to catch up with the other members of the group, who were standing bewildered and unsure of themselves on the pavement overlooking the Thames Embankment.

After apologising for the delay, and realising that, however much she might dislike Luke Cunningham, he'd been quite right about her running out of time, Angelica quickly shepherded her companions along to Chelsea Old Church. Fortunately, they were so interested in seeing the ancient bibles, with their original chains to prevent theft—the only ones still remaining in a London church—that they seemed prepared to forgive her bad timekeeping as she led them along Cheyne Walk, past the row of large, early-eighteenth-century houses overlooking the Thames, which had been lived in by so many famous people.

Since Lonsdale House was situated in the middle of the row, Angelica had her own very good reasons—mostly concerned with Luke Cunningham—for not wishing to linger any longer than necessary in Cheyne Walk. She was therefore horrified, when standing outside the house once lived in by the artist Dante Gabriel Rossetti, to see Betty Roberts' plump figure walking along the road towards them. Feeling quite faint with apprehension, Angelica quickly turned her back on the elderly woman, swiftly bringing her informative talk to a close, and briskly leading the group on to view the other houses once lived in by the prime minister David Lloyd George, and the Victorian authoress George Eliot.

Practically holding her breath, she peered anxiously back to see if Betty, who'd seemed to be carrying some bags of shopping, was intending to enter Lonsdale House or—she paled at the thought—continuing on up the road to visit some of her friends. Because once Betty spotted her there would be nothing to prevent Luke from adding up two and two to make four, and discovering not only her surname, but exactly where she lived.

Almost sagging with relief as she noticed, out of the corner of her eye, that Betty had stopped by the ornate wrought-iron gate leading to her home, Angelica suddenly realised that she'd been rejoicing too soon. Because Luke, who'd fallen slightly behind the group, was turning to stroll slowly back towards the elderly woman. Frozen with horror, Angelica could only stand helplessly by, holding her breath as she saw him begin to engage the housekeeper in conversation.

Realising that there was nothing she could do about the situation, Angelica took a deep breath and tried to concentrate on the job in hand, which was guiding her companions up Royal Hospital Road, before turning right into Swan Walk and the entrance to Chelsea Physic Garden.

Little known to the general public, the Physic Garden's three acres was one of Europe's oldest gardens. Founded in 1673, and a Mecca for those interested in the history of rare and medicinal plants, it also contained many unusual trees and flowers from all quarters of the globe. Over the centuries, the garden had played an important part in spreading the cultivation of plants and seeds to other countries, even sending the very first cotton seeds to America, to found the staple crop of what had been, at the time, the new colony of Georgia.

Relieved to have reached the end of a most exhausting walk, Angelica thankfully handed her group over to a member of the garden staff for the official tour, to be followed by tea in the lecture-room, and an opportunity to buy various plants and shrugs in the garden shop.

Although she was hardly an expert on gardening, Angelica was frequently drawn to the quiet, peaceful serenity of this leafy enclave, where the faint hum of bees and the rich scent of flowers could make the harsh, noisy city seem light-years away. And so, after paying the collective entrance fee for the group, and bidding them farewell, she slowly made her way down a tree-lined path towards the exit, deciding on the spur of the moment to sink down on to a wooden bench in a shady corner at the far end of the garden.

Just as she was beginning to relax, and congratu-
lating herself on having both survived the trauma
of a mentally exhausting tour, and also on managing to avoid any further contact with Luke
Cunningham, her period of quiet reflection was
abruptly shattered by the sudden appearance of his
tall figure.

'Ah—so that's where you've been hiding. I was
wondering where you'd got to,' he murmured,
ducking his dark head beneath the leafy overhead
boughs as he made his way towards her.

'Oh, no!' Angelica gave a heavy sigh. 'Why aren't
you with the others, having a tour of the garden?'

He shrugged. 'I got delayed. By the time I arrived, the rest of the group seemed deeply involved
in a discussion of various medicinal herbs—about
which I know very little, and care even less!'

'You're really missing something, because it's a
very interesting place,' she told him, trying to sound
wildly enthusiastic in the hope that he'd leave her
alone. But when he continued to stand looking
down at her, and clearly had no intention of taking
the broad hint, she asked him as casually as possible
why he'd fallen behind the other walkers.

'I was having a rather interesting talk with an
elderly lady, who told me that she lived in one of
the houses in Cheyne Walk. Apparently it also
functions as a somewhat unusual museum. Do you
know anything about it?'

'Me? Why on earth should I?' Angelica retorted
quickly, trying hard to quell her nerves as she
shrugged, and pretended that she hadn't any idea
of what he was talking about.

'You seem to know the area pretty well,' he pointed out. 'So I naturally assumed that you would know something about this small, local museum—even if it is only open one day a week.'

'Oh, well—it just goes to show that I've still got a lot to learn, doesn't it?' she replied carelessly, hoping against hope that Betty had, for once in her life, firmly kept her mouth shut about exactly *which* day they were open to the public. And then, as she noticed him staring down at her with an oddly intense, sceptical expression on his face, she quickly realised that she might have overdone her apparent casual lack of concern. This man was clearly no fool, and the sooner she changed the subject the better.

'Since you're clearly not interested in gardens or gardening, I can't think why you ever bothered to come on this walk in the first place. If you work in the City, what on earth are you doing in Chelsea?'

He gave a shrug of his broad shoulders. 'I decided to take some time off work. Also, as I'm sure you must have realised by now,' he added, coming over to sit down on the bench beside her, 'I'm obviously interested in furthering our—er—acquaintance.'

'I can't think why,' she muttered, nervously inching away from him. 'We've only met on two occasions. As far as I can see, that's clearly twice too many. In any case,' she added, hurriedly jumping to her feet, 'it really is time that I went home.'

'I have a car parked near by. I'd be happy to give you a lift.'

'No!' she gasped, before quickly trying to mask her horrified reaction with a hasty cough. 'I mean— um—I'm sure it's very kind of you, but there's really no need to bother.'

'It will be no bother at all,' he informed her firmly as he too rose slowly to his feet.

Feeling sick as she realised that she was well and truly stuck—and in a hole which she'd so stupidly dug for herself—Angelica couldn't seem to prevent all her deep, simmering resentments against this man from rising to the surface. Thanks to his baleful presence, it had been a long, mentally exhausting afternoon. And just when she'd thought that she had got rid of him, and was beginning to relax from all the stress and strain, he'd suddenly appeared—like the wicked ogre in a fairy-story— to pester and annoy her once again. It was just all too much!

'Look—why don't you go away and leave me alone?' she demanded angrily. 'You may be taking time off from your job, but the rest of us are still trying to earn a living as best we can. I'm not blind,' she added grimly. 'It's obvious that you're a wealthy man, and probably hold a senior position in your bank. Just as it's clearly obvious that you seem to be getting some kind of kick out of teasing me. And maybe it's partly my fault, because I very stupidly keep rising to the bait. But there are millions of other people living in Britain——' she waved her hands distractedly in the air '—so why don't you go off and plague the life out of one of them instead?'

'Yes, it would seem that I do owe you an apology.' The normally wry, sardonic note in his voice seemed curiously absent as he placed a warm hand beneath her chin, tilting her face up towards his.

'I'm not entirely sure what is happening between us,' he admitted slowly. 'Possibly it is just that I find your unusual personality very intriguing. After all, I cannot recollect ever being hailed as "sunshine" before. Nor am I used to having my shins kicked by a raging virago!' He smiled down at her. 'So you see, I'm almost as much out of my depth as you seem to be.'

He was barely touching her, but the light, soft feel of the fingers beneath her chin and the unusually warm, almost seductive tone in his deep voice seemed to be affecting her in an alarming manner. Her legs began to feel pathetically weak, and Angelica found that, quite inexplicably, she was suddenly feeling extraordinarily faint and breathless.

'I don't know what you're talking about,' she muttered helplessly, dimly realising that she ought to escape from this potentially fraught situation as quickly as possible. But it seemed as though she was temporarily paralysed by a strangely compelling, glittering light in the hooded grey eyes regarding her so intently. 'I ... I'm not out of my depth.'

He gave a husky bark of laughter. 'Oh, yes, my dear Angelica, you most certainly are. Why else should you be so on the defensive, so aggressively determined to fight me every inch of the way?' he murmured, his strong arms closing firmly about her quivering figure.

'You're quite...quite wrong! And this really isn't a good idea...' she whispered helplessly, her mind in total confusion as he lowered his dark head to within inches of her own.

'Whether it's good or bad, I can promise you that it's just about the *only* idea I've had all afternoon,' he breathed thickly.

The hard strength of the arms about her body, and the faintly elusive perfume of his cologne mingling with his own musky, masculine scent, seemed to pervade and overwhelm her senses. There was no sound other than the rustling leaves above her head, and she quite suddenly became shockingly aware of his vibrant, sexual attraction.

'You see what I mean...?' he whispered softly, glimpsing the sudden flicker of comprehension in her wide blue eyes. 'And, if it's any consolation to you, I appear to be infected by the same virus!'

The husky note of wry self-mockery in his voice seemed to linger in the air, echoing in her ears as his mouth possessed her trembling lips, teasing them apart with soft, gentle kisses. And then his arms tightened about her, moulding her body firmly to the hard length of his muscular figure, his kiss deepening as he sensually explored the inner softness of her mouth.

Almost faint with dizziness, her heart beating in a crazy, uneven rhythm as his seductive lips seemed to compel her to respond ardently and passionately to his lovemaking, Angelica found herself helplessly enmeshed by a force beyond her control. Winding her slim arms up about his neck, her fingers buried themselves convulsively in his thick, dark hair as she instinctively pressed herself closer to his powerful frame. Her action provoked a low groan from deep in his throat, his hands sweeping over the soft curves of her body, before lingering on the warm swell of her firm breasts.

Luke's lips seemed to linger reluctantly as they left her mouth, trailing down to the wildly beating pulse at the base of her throat. Slowly lifting his head, he gazed down at her with gleaming, enigmatic grey eyes, before raising a hand to remove the combs holding her hair in place on top of her head.

'It was the first thing that I noticed about you. I don't think I've ever seen such glorious hair!' he breathed, gently running his fingers through the long, pale, shimmering strands now tumbling down about her shoulders.

The husky, thickly muttered words seemed to come from a long way off as she found herself slowly surfacing from the deep mist of desire.

A moment later, her cheeks covered with a hot, fiery blush, Angelica realised that she'd just been kissing—with considerable enthusiasm and passion—a man who she was quite certain that she actively disliked. *How could she*? Was she entirely out of her mind? But maybe she was, because her body seemed to be shaking as if in the grip of a raging fever, while the seemingly unanswerable questions echoed in her head like the knell of doom.

Gazing down at the girl, whose bewilderment and confusion were clearly reflected in her distraught expression, Luke's firm lips twisted into a rueful smile.

'Maybe you were right to warn me? Maybe that kiss may prove to have been fatal, for us both...?'

he said slowly, bending down to brush his mouth gently once more over her trembling lips, before turning abruptly and striding swiftly away, his tall figure soon completely disappearing from sight.

Left standing alone in the quiet garden, Angelica staggered over to the bench on legs which felt as though they were made of cotton wool. Sinking slowly down on to the hard wooden seat, she stared blindly into space for a long, long time.

CHAPTER FOUR

ALTHOUGH Angelica liked to think that she was reasonably fit, the long climb up rickety stairs to David Webster's office always seemed to leave her with aching legs, and feeling considerably out of breath. Today was no exception, she thought wryly, rubbing her aching calf muscles as she waited for David to finish a conversation on the phone.

Situated up under the eaves of a tall City building, which must have been in existence well before Charles Dickens's day, the office of Footsteps in Time looked as if it, too, belonged to the early Victorian era. Piles of thick, dusty ledgers were stacked up against the walls, with David's desk an island encircled by open boxes of brochures, waste-paper baskets overflowing with rubbish, and chipped mugs still containing the stale dregs of tea and coffee which he'd consumed over the past week.

'Honestly, David—this place is absolutely disgusting!' she told him when he put down the receiver, wrinkling her nose at the cloud of dust filling the air as he dropped a set of large, heavy files on to the grubby carpet. 'Isn't it about time you found someone to give this place a good clean?'

He shrugged. 'I can't seem to find anyone who's prepared to climb up all these stairs. Besides, we can't all live in splendour in Cheyne Walk.' He raised his head to give her a brief grin, before con-

tinuing to hunt for a letter among the confusion of
files and papers on his desk.

'Ha, ha!' She grimaced, well aware of his forth-
right views on her home, which he'd frequently referred to in the past as 'an obsolete mausoleum'.
'I only wish it *were* splendid, because then we might
at least have some visitors to pay for the cost of its
upkeep. Do you know, we had a total of four people
last week—and three of them were only taking
shelter from a sudden rain shower?'

Angelica sighed, brushing a distracted hand
through her long hair. 'I hope you've got a lot of
work for me,' she continued, 'because the bills seem
to be mounting up so thick and fast that I'll have
to earn a fortune just to keep up with the payments.'

'Well ... keep this under your hat, but things
could be looking up.'

'Really?'

'Yes. I can't go into details just at the moment,
of course. But it looks as if I may be gaining a new
partner, and that means we could be doing a lot
more business in the near future.'

'Hey—that's great!' She grinned. 'I should have
realised, from the vague suggestion of a smile on
your normally miserable face, that something must
be up.'

'Thanks,' he muttered drily. 'Now, did you just
come here to trade insults, or do you have a
problem?'

'Well, it isn't *exactly* a problem,' she said slowly,
the smile dying on her face as she wondered how
to frame the question without going into a
long, involved explanation of why she needed
the information.

'The thing is, I'm not sure of our legal position—as far as the public is concerned, that is. It's all right, there's no need to panic,' she added quickly as he gazed at her in alarm, all trace of his previous good humour vanishing like snow in sunshine.

'Oh, Angelica!' he groaned. 'What on earth have you done *now*?'

'I haven't done anything!' she retorted indignantly. 'It's just that . . . well, someone on a walk I was leading the other day sort of—er—intimated that by taking their money, and issuing a receipt, we had come to some kind of deal, or contract. I just wondered if they were right—that's all.'

David relaxed slightly and leaned back in his chair. 'I'm no lawyer, of course, but I suppose it could possibly be regarded as a contract. However, it doesn't sound as if it's likely to be of any great importance.'

'But what happens if . . . well, let's say one of the group becomes extremely stroppy? I'm only talking hypothetically, of course,' she added hurriedly. 'But it does sometimes happen that a client turns out to be a real pain in the neck, right? So, could they sue me—or you, as my employer—because of a contract between us and them . . . if you see what I mean?'

'Oh, come on, Angelica—why should anyone want to sue us?'

'Well—um——' She gave a helpless shrug, gazing fixedly down at the desk as she desperately tried to think of a valid reason why any normal, rational person would bother to go to such lengths.

'With the walks only costing under five pounds a head, we're hardly talking about a fortune,' he pointed out, accurately echoing her own thoughts. 'However, I can see that it wouldn't do our business any good. What's brought this on, anyway? I don't like the sound of this "hypothetical" case. Are you *quite* sure that your last walk went smoothly? It was around Chelsea, wasn't it?' he added, flicking back through the pages of his diary.

'Why should there have been any problems?' she countered swiftly. Almost holding her breath, she added, 'You haven't had any complaints, have you?'

He shook his head. 'No. Although I will confess I was seriously worried about that trip around the City which you led last week. However, some woman rang up, wanting to know the date and place of your next tour—so you must have done a good job.'

'Oh—er—good,' she muttered, trying not to look too amazed, and hoping that the sudden rush of colour flooding over her pale cheeks might be mistaken for a modest blush of pleasure at what was, for David, high praise.

'However, if you *do* have any trouble with a member of the public, and you really feel that you can't cope with the situation, then all you have to do is to threaten to call a policeman. That generally does the trick.'

'Yes, I suppose so,' she sighed, realising that there was no way she could possibly even begin trying to explain the disturbing, traumatic series of events which had taken place lately. And exactly what a policeman could have done about Luke

Cunningham's devastating embrace, which had left her completely shattered, Angelica had absolutely no idea.

It was also extremely unlikely that David would be interested to know that she'd scarcely been able to get a wink of sleep since then. Or that when she did eventually manage to nod off she seemed to be haunted by a tall, dark figure stalking arrogantly through her dreams. The fact that she appeared to have completely lost her appetite wasn't exactly of earth-shattering importance, either.

If only there were someone she could talk to. Someone who might help to put the present phase of her life—which appeared to have been turned completely upside-down—into some sort of correct perspective. Unfortunately, the one person on whom she could always rely for hard, practical common-sense and good advice was away on holiday at the moment.

Angelica and Kim Edwards had become firm friends at school, before going on to university together, and were still staunch supporters of each other in good times as well as bad. It was unusual for a close friendship to last so long, but maybe it was because they were so different, both in looks and temperament. With her short, dark hair, practical, down-to-earth outlook, and a successful career running a modern art gallery, Kim's lifestyle was the very opposite of Angelica's. Even their homes reflected the dissimilarity between them, Kim's ultra-modern penthouse apartment in Chelsea Harbour being the total antithesis of Lonsdale House.

If only Kim weren't away in New York, and could give her some sensible, practical advice, maybe...

'Come on, Angelica—stop daydreaming!' David's exasperated voice broke into her dismal thoughts. 'If you haven't got any other queries, you'd better push off. I've got to get this new brochure finished and at the printers by this afternoon.

'Don't worry about difficult clients,' he called after her as she was closing the office door. 'As you know, they're a hazard of the trade. With our walks only taking about two hours, the best thing is just to grin and bear it. OK?'

'No, it definitely is *not* OK...!' Angelica muttered grumpily under her breath as she trailed slowly down the many flights of stairs.

It was all very well for David to say 'grin and bear it', but *he* hadn't been forced to put up with the sort of cataclysmic, horrendous turn of events which had afflicted her lately.

It wasn't just the sudden advent of Luke Cunningham into her life, and the devastating effect he seemed to be having on her emotions—although that was bad enough! But she hadn't been joking when she'd told David about her urgent need for money. After receiving the latest estimate from the builders, she had been forced to accept that the repairs to the roof timbers were likely to cost many thousands of pounds. She hadn't even a faint hope of raising that huge amount—not without some outside help and advice. On top of which, and adding yet another burden to her ever-mounting problems, her visit to Lady Marshall had proved to be an absolute disaster!

Unfortunately, Angelica knew that she had nobody but herself to blame. Confused and upset by her emotional encounter with Luke, it had been incredibly foolish of her to arrive on the old lady's doorstep in such a distraught state of mind. It would have been far more sensible to go straight home, where she could have phoned to cancel her visit, putting it off to another time. But when Luke had left her in the Physic Garden she'd been so shattered that she had hardly known what time of day it was, let alone been able to think clearly.

She had spent a long time searching in vain for her hair combs—which Luke had removed and thrown away. So, feeling completely disorientated and confused, she had not only arrived late, but also looking a complete and utter mess. Neither state was guaranteed to win the good opinion of the imperious old woman, who'd immediately launched into a lecture regarding modern-day dress and manners.

From that inauspicious beginning, the visit had proceeded rapidly downhill. Lady Marshall had forcibly spoken her mind about those who couldn't manage their finances correctly, and who must— for their own sakes, of course—be forced to economise in these hard times.

'There is absolutely no excuse for not having put aside money for the roof repairs,' the old woman had told her firmly. 'One must foresee the problems which lie ahead, and take adequate measures to see that they are catered for. After all, where would I be if I hadn't kept a sharp eye on my own investments?' she'd added, gazing down with satisfaction at the heavy gold and diamond rings on her fingers.

And exactly where would Lady Marshall have been without the rich legacy from her late husband, Sir Edward? Surely *that* question was more to the point? Angelica had thought grimly. And, while she didn't envy or resent the old lady's obvious wealth and comfort, she was desperate to try and save Lonsdale House—the only home she'd ever known.

Angelica always dreaded invitations to tea with the elderly woman. It meant hardly daring to move, just in case she should inadvertently disturb any of the precious glass and porcelain ornaments set out on the many small tables in the crowded drawing-room.

Lady Marshall's large house in Belgravia was crammed full of valuable antique furniture, paintings and *objets d'art*, which must have been an absolute nightmare to dust and clean. So it was fortunate that she could afford an army of servants, whom she kept busy from dawn to dusk.

Isolated from the real world, by having more than enough money to indulge her slightest whim, the old woman appeared to be totally out of touch with the ordinary, everyday problems of those who had to work for their living.

As she'd tried to explain, Angelica certainly wasn't afraid of hard work. But, while she had to look after and care for Lonsdale House, she had no way of earning any serious money. And she definitely didn't have the capital sums required to cover major items, such as the repairs to the roof timbers. However, since there was apparently plenty of money in the large trust fund, which was designed for just such a problem, it seemed only fair that the trustees should help her out during the present crisis.

But she might as well have saved her breath. Lady Marshall either couldn't or wouldn't understand the problem. It was only when Angelica realised that it was pointless to keep on trying to get the message over, and was rising to leave, that the old woman had made even the slightest offer of help.

'I will contact a young niece of my dear late husband,' she'd told Angelica, ringing for the aged butler to show her visitor out. 'I understand that she now holds a senior position in a firm of accountants. Maybe she will be able to suggest an answer to this deplorable situation.'

That disastrous visit to the imperious old lady had been a complete waste of time, Angelica now told herself unhappily, trailing slowly down the last steps of the tall office building, and out into the busy street. Maybe she should just give up, and stop trying to persuade the trustees to advance money for the urgent repairs to Lonsdale House?

She was so immersed in her miserable thoughts that it wasn't until she collided with someone that she came down to earth—literally with a bump!

'Whoops! Sorry, Angelica.' Her colleague, Grog Harper, grinned as he bent down to help her up off the pavement, where she'd fallen after the collision with his tall figure. 'Are you all right?'

'Yes, I think so,' she muttered, brushing the dust off her blue checked shirt and denim jeans.

She was very fond of Grog, who was easily the most successful tour guide working for Footsteps in Time. His walk *On the Trail of Jack the Ripper* was always a smash hit with the public. Taking place in the evening, and evoking the menacing atmosphere of Victorian London, with its fog and gas lights, frightening shadows and stealthy footsteps, he would lead his companions through the various series of murders in the East End of London.

'How did you get on with your tour around the City last week?' he queried as she dusted herself down.

'Don't ask!' Angelica groaned.

'It can't have been that bad, surely?'

'Oh, yes, it was. To be honest—and for goodness' sake, *please* don't tell David—I have to admit that it was an absolute fiasco!' she told him ruefully.

'What went wrong?'

'Just about everything,' she admitted gloomily. 'And, just to make everything ten times worse, I had a real Mr Know-all along who made my life a complete misery.'

'That was bad luck,' he agreed with a sympathetic smile. 'But I'm sure you'll have managed to cope with him.'

'Er…well…' she mumbled, her cheeks flushing as she swiftly decided that she didn't want to get into any further discussion about the disastrous tour. In fact, it was definitely time to change the subject. 'So—what are you doing here?'

He shrugged. 'Nothing much. David seems to be quite excited about someone who's apparently injecting a large amount of capital into the business. So I was popping in to see if he's intending to make any radical changes to the programme.'

'Yes, David did drop a few heavy hints that the business might be expanding very soon. He certainly seemed unusually cheerful.'

'That will make a pleasant change!' Grog laughed. 'I'm also calling in to check the details of a new tour I've been putting together. I thought it might be fun to do a Sherlock Holmes walk, visiting some of the places mentioned in Conan Doyle's stories. I've been trying to think of a title, but I'm a bit stuck. Any ideas?'

'How about *Elementary, My Dear Watson . . .*?'

'Not bad—not bad at all!' He grinned. 'In fact, I think I might try that out on David. Well done, Angelica!' he added, enveloping her slim form in a huge bear hug, before going upstairs to see their employer.

It must have been her overwrought imagination at work again, Angelica told herself as she travelled home on the bus. Because, just as she was being given such an enthusiastic, friendly hug by Greg, she'd been almost certain that on glancing over his shoulder she had caught sight of Luke Cunningham. But she *must* have been mistaken, she told herself quickly. It had only been a brief, fleeting glimpse of a man frowning at her and Greg from the back of a long black chauffeur-driven limousine as it travelled swiftly down the street. It could . . . well, it could have been just about anyone, she told herself firmly, terrified by the way that Luke's powerful, dark presence seemed to be invading her waking hours now, as well as dominating her dreams.

However, the very next day, when Lonsdale House was open to the public, Angelica's sinking

heart knew that this time she couldn't blame her
overheated imagination. The tall figure, now
walking up the steps and confidently striding into
the main hall of her home, really *was* Luke
Cunningham!

It seemed to take an age before the message con-
veyed by her eyes managed to reach her frozen
brain. As if in a trance, her limbs frozen with shock
and horror, all she could think of was that—like
some evil magician—Luke seemed to be able to
materialise suddenly out of thin air. And then her
mind was filled by the imperative question: how on
earth had he managed to discover where she lived?

On her return to the house after visiting Lady
Marshall, Angelica had tried to discover from Betty
exactly what she'd said to Luke when he'd stopped
to talk to her during the tour of Chelsea. But Betty
hadn't been able to understand her urgent need to
know the worst.

'What is this—the third degree?' the elderly
woman had demanded irritably. 'For goodness'
sake, Angelica! How can I be expected to remember what I did or didn't say? And why are you
so interested, anyway? All *I* know is that he seemed
a very nice gentleman,' Betty had told her, before
flouncing off down into the kitchen.

Now, clutching the back of a nearby chair for
support, Angelica gazed with stunned eyes at the
'very nice gentleman' as she desperately tried to pull
herself together.

'Good afternoon, Angelica,' he murmured,
looking about him with interest.

'W-what...?' she croaked, her legs suddenly
feeling as though they were about to give way be-

neath her. Taking a deep breath, she tried again. 'What...what are you doing here?'

He raised a dark, quizzical eyebrow as her low, husky voice echoed eerily around the large hall.

'My dear girl—what does it look as if I'm doing?' he drawled, moving over to gaze up at a painting on the wall. 'I'm here to see over Sir Tristram Lonsdale's house and to view his collection, of course.'

'But how...why...?'

'Because it's the only day in the week when you're open to the public,' he pointed out patiently, as if talking to a particularly dim-witted child.

'I don't need you to tell me that!' she snapped. 'But I still don't understand. I mean, how did you...?'

'How did I discover where you lived?' He gave a short bark of sardonic laughter. 'Oh, come on! Did you *really* think that I wouldn't be able to find out?'

Since that was exactly what she'd thought and hoped, she could only stare back at him with fear and trepidation. Tongue-tied, the knuckles of her hand whitening as her grip tightened on the chair rail, Angelica struggled to try and pull herself together.

Quite apart from the sheer embarrassment of the situation—her cheeks flamed at the memory of what had happened when they'd last met—she still couldn't believe what was happening to her. It was so unfair to find, after all the trouble she'd taken to prevent him learning her address, that she might as well have spared herself the effort.

The hall was large for a London town house, and yet it now seemed filled with his dominant presence. He must spend a fortune on his clothes, she told herself grimly, staring over at the tall, lean figure wearing an impeccably cut, lightweight grey suit, the white silk shirt emphasising his tanned features and the thick, dark hair just touching his collar. However, despite his usual immaculate appearance, Angelica instinctively knew that it would be a great mistake to ignore the lean, muscular, hard strength beneath his expensive clothes. Because, as she was at last beginning to realise, Luke Cunningham was both a dangerous and very determined man.

'Well?'

'Hmm . . .?' She looked up to find him regarding her with some amusement.

'I presume that you do charge an entrance fee?' he said, reaching inside his jacket and producing a wallet.

She nodded, and then found herself becoming confused and flustered when he placed a large note in her shaking hands, waving away her attempt to give him his change.

'Well—er—in that case you'd better have a free brochure,' she muttered, nervously stuffing it into his hands as two middle-aged ladies entered the hall.

Busy dealing with the newcomers, Angelica had a few moments to realise that there was very little, if anything, she could do about the situation.

Although the idea of attempting to evict Luke forcibly had flickered briefly through her mind, she had almost immediately abandoned the idea. Not only were there now two witnesses to any action

that she might take, but she could hardly do anything on her own. And, with Betty busy downstairs
in the kitchen baking cakes for a church bazaar,
her next idea—of disappearing upstairs to her
bedroom, and staying there until he left—was also
quickly discarded. Someone had to be on duty and,
as Luke had reminded her, he was a member of the
public. He had, therefore, a perfect right to walk
around the house if he chose to do so.

However, as it soon became apparent, that wasn't
enough for him. Oh, no! Luke, it seemed, was determined to have his pound of flesh as well.

'I see from this brochure that you do conducted
tours. I think I'd like that,' he told her blandly.
And despite her obvious reluctance to conduct him
anywhere—other than out of the front door!—it
looked as though she hadn't any choice but to
comply.

There seemed no way of avoiding this fraught,
difficult situation, until she turned her eyes on the
two middle-aged ladies. If she was being forced to
conduct a tour around the house, there was nothing
that said how many people should or should not
be included in the group. Quickly making up her
mind, she went over to the woman, asking if they
were interested in being shown personally around
the various artefacts and curiosities.

While in actual fact it didn't take very long, it
seemed to Angelica as though it was hours and
hours before she led her three visitors back into the
hall.

'Thank you so much—it was all very—er—very
interesting,' one of the ladies said kindly as Angelica
escorted them towards the front door.

Impatiently waiting for Luke to join them, and looking forward to getting rid of the man at last, Angelica was thrown when he suddenly murmured, 'I think I'll just take another look at one of the paintings in the dining-room.'

After seeing the women off the premises, she hurried back to the hall, nonplussed on reaching the oak-panelled dining-room to find that there was no sign of Luke. Hunting feverishly through the other rooms on the ground floor, she quickly ran out into the garden, and then up the wide staircase to see if, by any chance, he'd sneaked upstairs when she wasn't looking. But there was no sign of his tall figure—either there, or in any of the bedrooms on the upper two floors. Not, of course, that she'd expected to find him up there—but she'd had to make sure, if only for her own peace of mind.

So where *was* the damned man? It wasn't as though he'd appeared to be at all interested in the contents of the house, she reminded herself with a puzzled frown, trailing slowly back down the staircase into the hall. The blank and impassive, almost deadpan expression on his face during the tour, during which he'd said virtually nothing, had proved to be considerably off-putting. There had been something particularly unnerving about his silent lack of response to what she'd been saying. In fact, Angelica had been grateful to the two middle-aged ladies for asking a few pertinent questions every now and then.

The main impression she'd gained was that Luke had been bored out of his mind by all the weird and strange exhibits. And if so, well, that was just too bad. It served him right for putting in an appearance where he clearly wasn't wanted! she told herself grimly, slowly making her way down to join Betty in the kitchen. With any luck, she'd never have to see him again. And surely the passing of time would help to banish those disturbing, erotic dreams which had been giving her so much trouble?

In the meantime, it was just a case of mind over matter, she told herself bracingly. She must concentrate on dismissing the whole unfortunate series of events from her mind. After all, she had plenty of other problems to think about at the moment, and...

'So *that's* where you've got to!' She glared angrily across the large old kitchen at Luke, who was quite calmly sitting at the scrubbed pine table. 'What the hell do you think you're doing?'

'What does it look as if I'm doing?' He grinned, taking another hefty bite from the large, thick slice of bread in his hand. 'Thanks to wonderful Mrs Roberts here...'

'There's no need to be so formal—just call me Betty,' the elderly woman urged, beaming down at him with what Angelica could only think of as a sickly, simpering smile.

'OK, Betty.' He grinned up at the housekeeper, who was standing beside the table carving thick slices of crusty bread from a large loaf. Turning his amused gaze on the rigidly angry girl, he added, 'Betty has been allowing me to sample some of her delicious home-made strawberry jam. I can tell you, it's really great!'

'You've absolutely no right to be down here!' Angelica ground out furiously. Her anger almost reached boiling-point as she saw her old nanny—

the traitor!—happily cutting into a freshly baked chocolate cake, smothered in thick chocolate icing, which had originally been destined for the church bazaar. 'This kitchen is *definitely* off-limits to the general public!'

'Really, Angelica! Whatever has happened to your manners?' Betty gasped, staring over at her with astonishment.

'OK, I'll plead guilty—and take the rap!' Luke held up his hands in mock-surrender. 'But in my defence I must tell you that I was nearly driven mad when you were conducting us around the house. I couldn't resist the wonderful smell drifting upstairs from this kitchen. Because if there's one thing I adore it's a freshly baked chocolate cake! It takes me right back to my childhood,' he added, giving Betty a warm smile as he sank his teeth into the succulent sponge. 'Umm...this is *terrific*!' he mumbled.

'Oh, good—I *am* pleased to hear that,' Angelica ground out sarcastically. 'Isn't there anything else you fancy? Some jam tarts? Or maybe you'd like a slice of lemon sponge cake? Of course, Betty has made them for the church bazaar—but I'm sure the vicar won't mind you scoffing the lot!'

Luke grinned and shook his dark head. 'It's a crime to allow this wonderful woman—a pearl among cooks—to squander her talent on a church sale. So, while I'll write him a large cheque for the restoration fund, or whatever, I'm afraid it's tough luck on the vicar!'

'Oh, great! You obviously believe a large cheque can solve everything!'

'Yes, it generally does solve most of life's problems,' he drawled sardonically.

'Now, stop squabbling, you two,' Betty said in a firm, nanny-like tone of voice. 'And you just calm down,' she added, turning to the girl trembling with rage on the other side of the room.

'I'm perfectly calm!' Angelica retorted through clenched teeth.

'Well, there's no need to get on your high horse, because it's nothing but a pleasure to feed a man who appreciates good, honest food.' Betty smiled down at Luke. 'It certainly makes a change from those little bits of salad, which is all I can seem to get you to eat these days. And I've a perfect right to feed anyone I want to, in my own kitchen,' the older woman added aggressively, before giving Luke another beaming smile.

The damned man wasn't just hijacking her life, he was also deliberately inveigling himself into her home and family, Angelica thought bitterly, noticing that Luke had removed the smart jacket of his suit, the sleeves of his white shirt rolled up to display his strong, tanned forearms lightly covered with dark hair.

And, more than just making himself comfortably at home in her house, he was also busy spreading his oily charm all over the kitchen. He'd certainly managed to turn the head of her old nanny—who was all the family that she had left, now that her grandmother was dead. How could Betty be so stupid as to fall for that outrageous flattery? Angelica asked herself, almost screaming with frustration as she saw the older woman happily cut him yet another slice of rich chocolate cake.

Unfortunately it looked as if there was nothing she could do about the situation. Short of bashing him about the head with one of the large copper saucepans, there seemed absolutely no way of getting rid of the awful man!

CHAPTER FIVE

'FOR goodness' sake, girl! Come and sit down. There's no point in standing over there like Joan of Arc at the stake,' Betty said firmly. 'What you need is a nice cup of tea.'

If Angelica hadn't been feeling so cross, she might have found it amusing to be addressed by her old nanny as if she were still in the nursery. But, furious with Luke, and outraged at his invasion of her private domain, she realised that she'd temporarily lost her sense of humour.

However, after a fierce internal struggle, she could see that there was little point in continuing to try and evict this man. He was clearly intending to ignore the fact that he wasn't wanted at Lonsdale House. Or not by her, at least. Unfortunately, it looked as though Betty—who'd always been susceptible to men with charm and a handsome face— had been bowled over by their visitor.

With a heavy sigh, Angelica shrugged before trailing slowly across the floor. It seemed that there was nothing she could do. Yet again, Luke Cunningham had somehow managed to out-manoeuvre her.

Pulling out a chair, she deliberately avoided looking at him as she sat down at the large kitchen table, covered with a red and white gingham tablecloth.

'Our *uninvited* visitor may be overdosing on your chocolate cake, but he was clearly bored out of his mind by Sir Tristram's collection,' she told Betty sourly.

'And who could blame him?' the older woman retorted. 'I reckon there must be centuries of dust on some of those curios. Besides, you know my views about that Egyptian mummy—nasty, un-hygienic thing! Did you see the mummified cat?' she asked Luke. 'What a way to treat a poor, dumb animal, even if it was dead at the time. Disgraceful, I call it!'

He smiled and shook his head. 'No, I'm afraid that I didn't notice the cat. However, Angelica is quite wrong,' he added, turning his hooded grey eyes on the stormy expression of the girl sitting across the table. 'I wasn't bored by all those crazy things upstairs. In fact, I was amused and intrigued by a great many of the objects.'

'Oh, yes? You could have fooled me!'

'But, as it stands, I'm afraid that you've got a fairly hopeless set-up,' he continued smoothly, ig-noring Angelica's derisory words. 'There are far too many articles on display, with no order or organ-isation to help your visitors. As for that brochure you've produced—I have to say that it's absolutely hopeless!'

'Thanks a bunch!' Angelica ground out sarcas-tically. 'Anything else you'd like to say, while you're about it?'

'Yes, as it happens—quite a lot,' he drawled. 'But maybe I'd better save it for another time?'

'Believe me, there isn't going to *be* another time!' she snapped angrily, prevented from giving any further expression to her injured feelings by Betty, who clearly believed in getting down to the basic nitty-gritty of a situation as soon as possible.

'Maybe your wife would like this recipe . . . ?' the older woman asked Luke, placing yet another slice of cake on his plate.

All those present in the kitchen were aware that the question, hovering delicately in the air, had absolutely nothing to do with a recipe. Angelica almost cringed with embarrassment at Betty's blatant attempt to discover Luke's marital status. And she was only too well aware of his lips twitching with suppressed laughter.

'I'd be pleased to give it to my wife,' he said, pausing for a moment before giving a clearly false mournful shake of his head. 'Unfortunately, I'm sorry to say that I'm not married.'

'Oh, really?' the older woman beamed down at him. 'Never mind, dear, I expect you'll soon find a nice girl to look after you.'

Angelica gave a high-pitched, scornful laugh. 'Not if she's got any sense, he won't!'

'That's not a very nice thing to say,' Betty told her with a frown, clearly worried that her attempts at matchmaking were going sadly astray.

'That's OK, I've a broad back,' Luke murmured with a heavily dramatic sigh, before turning to the older woman and asking plaintively, 'Tell me, is she always this bad-tempered?'

Betty shook her head. 'Oh, no, she's normally a lovely girl. But I must admit that she does seem to have been a bit emotionally upset lately.'

Oh, for heaven's sake! Angelica was bitterly aware of a hot tide of crimson sweeping over her pale cheeks. She dearly loved Betty—but just at this precise moment she could have cheerfully *murdered* her old nanny! It didn't need a swift glance at the sardonic glint in Luke's eyes to realise that he was enjoying her embarrassment. Not to mention the fact that the insufferably arrogant, conceited man obviously believed that *he* was responsible for her recent emotional disturbance. An assumption that was, of course, complete and utter nonsense!

'Do you mind?' she snapped irritably. 'I'd be grateful if you'd both kindly *not* discuss me as if I'm some sort of strange animal. And stop laughing at me, you horrid man, or I really will lose my temper!' she suddenly found herself yelling at Luke, who was now leaning back in his chair, his shoulders shaking with amusement.

As her ears filled with the sound of her angry outburst echoing around the kitchen, and she caught sight of the expression of shock on Betty's face, she flushed again with shame and mortification.

'OK, I'm sorry,' she mumbled, staring down at the checked tablecloth. 'I shouldn't have shouted like that.'

'Quite right—you ought to be ashamed of yourself,' Betty said, rubbing salt in the wound. 'However, it's time I had my afternoon nap. So I'll leave you two to sort matters out. But if you *must* quarrel with one another,' she added in nanny-like tones as she walked over to the door, 'kindly have the goodness to keep your voices down!'

There was a long silence following the older woman's departure from the kitchen, which was finally broken by Luke's clearing his throat.

'I think it might be a good idea to forget the past few minutes and to start again, don't you?'

'Yes, all right...' Angelica muttered with a defensive shrug, avoiding his eyes as she stared blindly down at the table.

'I'm intrigued by this beautiful, old and rather weird house,' he continued, taking no notice of her unenthusiastic reply. 'You obviously didn't believe me, but I meant it when I said that I'd enjoyed looking around the exhibition.'

'Really...?' She surveyed him warily.

'Yes—really,' he smiled. 'But, as things stand at the moment, it seems that you've got some serious problems. Can we agree on that, at least?'

'I suppose so,' she murmured cautiously, with another shrug of her slim shoulders, determined not to let Luke see that even one careless smile from him could wreak havoc with her equilibrium.

'Right. Now, as I see the situation, you two ladies are living in this house, and opening it up to the public once a week. You also make a small charge for admission. However, since you rarely have more than a handful of visitors at any one time, this place can hardly even begin to pay its way, let alone bring you in a decent income. Am I correct?'

Angelica slowly nodded. 'That seems to be a masterly summing-up of the present situation,' she grudgingly admitted. 'There is the trust fund, of course. But trying to get any money from the trustees, who have plenty of funds available, is like trying to get blood from a stone. They just don't seem to understand that I can't afford to pay for all the problems with the roof. I honestly don't know *what* I'm going to do,' she added with a heavy sigh.

'Whoa—hang on a moment,' Luke said, taking a small notebook from his jacket pocket. 'I think you'd better explain about this trust. How and when was it formed? And who are the trustees?'

It was probably a complete waste of time, but Angelica found it a considerable relief to be able to talk frankly about her problems. And, while Luke said very little other than to ask one or two pertinent questions, he seemed to have an immediate grasp and understanding of her difficult financial situation.

'OK, let's see if I've got this right,' he said at last, when she'd explained the historical background to the present state of affairs. 'As I understand it, your family has lived in this house since the eighteenth century—ever since it was inherited by a distant relative of Sir Hans Sloane. Is that Sloane as in Sloane Square?'

Angelica nodded. 'Sir Hans Sloane was an amazing man. A very rich physician, and doctor to both Samuel Pepys and Queen Anne, he travelled all over the world collecting plants and fossils, coins, books, ancient statues and manuscripts. In fact when he died, aged ninety-three, his collection formed the basis of what is now the British Museum.'

'So the relative was left this house, and also some of the minor pieces from Sloane's collection which weren't considered good enough for the British Museum. And then what?'

'Well, nothing much, really,' she shrugged. 'The house stayed in the family through various generations, until they all died off, leaving only a wealthy young orphan, Angelica—after whom I'm named. She married Tristram Lonsdale, but died soon after giving birth to their only son. So Sir Tristram became a very rich man, even before he'd begun making his own fortune as a painter.'

Luke frowned. 'I've now got a picture of the background. But, without actually going through the accounts with a magnifying glass, it seems there must be plenty of money in the trust fund.' He shrugged. 'Trustees can sometimes be difficult, of course. But in this case I can't really see the problem.'

'There was no problem until my grandmother died,' Angelica told him sadly, before relating the troublesome situation which had arisen over her shared inheritance. 'Unfortunately, no one can seem to find any trace of the lady—a Mrs Eastman, who apparently lives in America. So the trustees have got the whip hand over me. They can't actually kick me out of the house, but they can—and do—make my life very difficult. If only I could get together with the missing lady, we could maybe break the trust. Or at least make sure that there isn't a problem about essential repairs.'

Luke's figure had become very still, staring down in deep concentration at the notes he'd made on the pad of paper in front of him.

'That still doesn't solve your problem with the layout and management of the collection upstairs,' he said at last. 'I really wasn't trying to tease you, or to be unkind,' he added with a sympathetic smile, 'but it truly is a mess and needs to be totally revamped.'

'Yes, I know it does,' she admitted, suddenly feeling hopelessly weak and breathless at the unexpected warmth of his smile. 'In fact, we really need an experienced curator to bring the museum up to date. But I haven't a hope of paying anyone a salary at the moment.'

'Hmm... I'll have to give your problem some considerable thought,' he said, making more notes on the pad before slipping it back in his pocket.

Realising that she hadn't explained her extra problems with Lady Marshall, Angelica was just about to do so when he glanced down at his watch and announced that he would have to leave.

'I'm sorry that I can't stay any longer,' he murmured as she led him back up the stairs and across the hall towards the front door. 'However, don't worry. I'm sure that I can come up with a solution to your difficulties.'

Although it had been therapeutic to be able to talk to Luke about her problems, Angelica was now beginning to realise that she might have made a grave mistake.

While it had been very kind of Luke to listen to her tale of woe, there was clearly little or nothing he could do about the situation. So what was the point of remaining in contact with the man? Especially when she found his strong, masculine aura and arrogant self-possession so overwhelmingly daunting.

Let's face it, she told herself roughly, you've no idea how to cope with this man. A man who had only to turn his cool grey eyes in her direction to have her either spitting with fury or swept by an inexplicable, crazy desire to throw herself into his arms.

Suddenly panic-stricken at the direction her thoughts were taking, Angelica was grateful for the subdued lighting in the hall, hoping that it would hide the hot, hectic flush she could feel sweeping over her pale cheeks. Placing a trembling hand on the latch of the front door, she took a deep breath and turned to face Luke.

'Thank you for being so kind, and having the patience to listen to my small—er—minor worries,' she muttered awkwardly.

'On the contrary, they are neither small nor minor. And I shall certainly do what I can to help you find a solution to your problems.'

She gulped nervously at the firm resolve underlying his words. 'I . . . I'm sure that you mean well, and I really don't want to seem ungrateful, but I can't see any point in your becoming involved. I mean, there's nothing you can do, and . . . well, it just seems a complete waste of your—er—valuable time,' she added lamely.

He stood staring down in silence at her for a moment. His granite-hard grey eyes regarded her from beneath their heavy eyelids with a deep, searching intensity which she found distinctly unnerving.

It seemed almost unbelievable that only a few minutes ago she'd been sitting in the kitchen with this man and calmly discussing her financial problems. She hadn't been frightened or worried then. Why should she now feel so nervous—almost threatened by the tall figure who was standing uncomfortably close beside her?

The atmosphere in the still, quiet hall suddenly seemed to become thick and heavy. She could almost physically feel the increasing aura of menace, pressing hard down on her slim shoulders. Surely he must be able to hear her loudly beating heart as it pounded heavily in her chest?

'I wonder why you're so frightened of me?' he drawled softly, raising his hand and trailing a finger gently down her pale cheek.

'Me—frightened?' She gave a strangled, incredulous laugh, jerking her head away from his light touch as if she'd been stung by a bee. 'Why on earth should I be frightened of you?'

'Why, indeed?' he agreed smoothly.

'You're quite wrong,' she told him as firmly as she could. Determinedly avoiding his eyes, she stared fixedly at a hunting print on the wall beside his broad shoulder.

'Well, in that case, why don't I come by later and take you out to dinner?'

Her immediate, instinctive response to his smoothly drawled invitation should have been a definite 'no'. So why on earth was she hesitating? she screamed silently to herself.

She didn't want to know this man. Ever since their very first, disastrous encounter, he'd succeeded in making her look a complete fool. And even in his absence he appeared to be having a thoroughly disconcerting and unsettling effect on her normally quiet, peaceful life. Moreover, she was—yes, she could at least admit it to herself— she definitely *was* frightened of him. Quite why he should be the cause of her feeling such anxiety and terror whenever she found herself alone with him she had absolutely no idea.

'Well—have we got a date?'

It might have seemed as though he was asking a question, but the cool, flat note of certainty and confidence in Luke's voice made it sound like a firm statement of fact.

'No!' she gasped quickly, hunting desperately in her mind for a reasonable excuse. And then she suddenly realised there was no point in trying to be polite. Only the hard, unvarnished truth would persuade this man that he was wasting his time.

'Look, I'm sorry that you're forcing me to be so blunt, but the truth is that I . . . I really don't want to have anything more to do with you. I realise that you may find it difficult to believe, but . . .'

'Yes, I do find it a little strange,' he agreed coolly. 'Especially when I remember just how enthusiastically you melted into my arms the last time we met. In fact, I have no problem in recalling the softness of your lips, or the warmth of your——'

'*Please*! I don't want even to *think* about it!' she wailed, frantically wishing that a large hole would appear in the floor and she could immediately disappear from sight.

'How very unfortunate!' He gave a low, mocking laugh. 'Because I, on the other hand, have thought of little else. In fact, Angelica,' he added wryly, 'I very much fear that you are responsible for upsetting all my carefully laid plans, as well as having a thoroughly distracting effect on my normally well-organised professional life!'

'But can't you see that I . . . I don't want to be responsible for anything of the sort?' she cried helplessly, a brilliant tide of colour staining her cheeks. 'I mean, I don't understand what keeps happening each time we meet...'

'Have you thought that maybe it's not me, but your own emotions of which you are clearly so afraid?' he taunted softly, the now unmistakable gleam in his eyes causing her to take a quick, nervous step backwards.

'No!' she gasped as he moved towards her, and she could read his intention as if he'd shouted the words out loud.

Her husky denial merely caused him to raise one dark eyebrow in mocking amusement. A brief moment later, his hands were reaching out to clasp her slim waist, pulling her reluctant figure slowly towards him.

'Stop fighting me, Angelica,' he breathed huskily, drawing her closer to the hard warmth of his body.

Trembling like a leaf as she attempted to control a mad, crazy urge to melt up against his strong, masculine figure, she raised her hands to try and push him away. But, as she already knew, he possessed a strength she simply wasn't able to combat. She could feel his hard, muscular thighs pressing against her own, and was conscious of a fierce knot of excitement in the pit of her stomach. Quivering, she stared helplessly up at his mouth as the dark head moved slowly down towards her. And then, from the moment his lips touched hers, it felt as though she was in the grip of a whirlwind of over-whelming emotion, responding blindly to the en-ticing magic of his deepening kiss.

It seemed as if she was totally bewitched. Unable to prevent herself from pressing her slim form even closer to him, her arms wound themselves about his neck; wild tremors of sensual excitement and pleasure flared through her trembling figure at the sound of his deep, muffled groan, provoked by the yielding softness of the body clasped so tightly in his arms.

She had no idea of how long they stood there in the hall. But slowly and reluctantly he eventually lifted his head, gazing down at her swollen lips and the confused, fluttering eyelashes over her dazed blue eyes.

He brushed his warm lips over her hotly flushed cheek. 'I find you very, very desirable,' he whispered huskily. 'In fact, it must be obvious by now that I'm crazy about you!' Wry humour gleamed in his eyes, his mouth curving into a sardonic smile. 'Isn't it about time, Angelica, that you faced the fact that you're crazy about me, too...?'

It was a moment or two before his words managed to break through the mist in her confused mind. And then, almost before she knew what she was doing, Angelica had pushed him away and was quickly pulling open the front door.

'No! No, I'm *not* crazy about you!' she panted breathlessly. 'I...I don't know what's wrong with me—maybe I'm sickening for something?—but I *do* know that this has got to stop. Now please go away and leave me alone!' she cried, clinging helplessly to the heavy oak door for support, her trembling legs threatening to give way beneath her any moment.

Luke appeared to be completely unperturbed by her outburst, merely giving an amused, cynical shrug of his broad shoulders as he moved past her through the open doorway.

'I don't mind you trying to fool me—even if it is a complete waste of time. But if you're trying to fool yourself, Angelica, I can't help feeling that you are making a great mistake,' he drawled sardonically. The sound of his mocking laughter as he ran down the steps echoed harshly in her ears long after she'd slammed the door behind him.

The string quartet playing in a small room off the main hall could hardly be heard above the general babble of conversation, laughter and the loud clink of glasses.

Moving slowly up the staircase and admiring the vivid dark blue tiles on the wall, Angelica had no doubt that the party to launch this exhibition— 'Three Eminent Victorian Artists—Landseer, Leighton and Lonsdale'—was proving to be a great success.

She knew very little of the work of Sir Edwin Landseer—although, of course, she'd seen the four bronze lions which he'd designed for the base of Nelson's Column in Trafalgar Square. Nor had she known very much about the Victorian painter, Lord Frederick Leighton. But now, standing in his remarkable house in Holland Park—the plain exterior giving no clue to the rich, highly ornate decoration inside—Angelica could see how the two artists and their paintings, together with those by Sir Tristram Lonsdale, could form the basis for this exhibition.

While the style and subject matter of their paintings had been very different, they'd all been

favourite artists of Queen Victoria, who had pur-
chased many of their paintings. They had also been
knighted by the Queen—although Frederick
Leighton had gone one better by being raised to the
peerage—unfortunately only one day before he
died! And this party, to launch an exhibition of the
three men's work arranged upstairs in the large art
gallery off Lord Leighton's enormous studio, had
attracted a great number of people, with many of
the guests spilling out into the wide green lawns of
the large garden.

Not that she knew anyone here, of course. But
since the organisers had borrowed some of Sir
Tristram's paintings from Lonsdale House, they
had been anxious that she should attend the party.
And she was glad to have done so, since she
wouldn't otherwise have had an opportunity to view
what must surely be one of the most exotic rooms
in London.

Accepting another glass of wine from a passing
waiter as she made her way through the crowd of
people, Angelica entered a tiny gallery off the upper
landing. Sinking down on to the jewelled silk
cushions which lined the small space, and opening
one of the delicate lattice screens, she peered down
at the room far below.

The Arab Hall had been designed as a showcase
for Lord Leighton's collection of antique, richly
glowing blue and green tiles, collected during his
travels in the Far East in the mid-1850s. Lining the
walls, they were topped by a wide, gilt mosaic frieze,
glittering and sparkling in the lamplight, which cast
mysterious shadows on the mosaic floor sur-
rounding a black marble fountain, the cool, tinkling

flow of water now hardly able to be heard above the buzz of conversation and laughter.

It was an amazing sight, evoking an extraordinarily Oriental *'Arabian Nights'* atmosphere of mystery and romance, especially when viewed from above in this small gallery, through the delicate lattice screens which had come from some ancient Arabian harem.

Open daily to the public, this amazingly flamboyant house was still redolent of its original owner's taste and personality, and Angelica was so thankful that she had decided to come here tonight, after all.

For the past two weeks, she'd been very reluctant to go anywhere, or to do anything. Following Luke's departure, when she'd virtually thrown him out of Lonsdale House following that last, passionate encounter in the hall, she had seen nothing of the disturbing man. And, although it had been several days before she'd managed to stop jumping nervously whenever she glimpsed a tall and dark-haired man, Angelica was now beginning to feel able to relax. It looked as though her blunt, almost cruel words of dismissal had finally made it absolutely clear that she wished to have no more to do with him.

Leaning back against the plump silk cushions, she sipped her glass of wine and tried to sort out the emotional muddle in which she now found herself. It sometimes felt as if she was trapped on a perpetual see-saw of indecision, her thoughts and desires fluctuating up and down until she was almost dizzy. For instance, she wondered with a heavy sigh, why, when she really *had* done the right thing, should her life now seem so incredibly dark and empty without Luke's strong, forceful presence?

Being sensible was all very well, but it didn't seem to be any help in the small hours of the night, when she longed desperately to have his strong arms about her once more. And continually reminding herself that Luke might be handsome, rich, attractive and God's gift to women, but as far as she was concerned he embodied nothing but trouble and aggravation, didn't seem to help at all.

On the other hand...how could she possibly trust a man who possessed such overwhelming charm? He'd had Betty eating out of his hand almost at the speed of light. And even she herself had repeatedly fallen a willing victim to his overwhelming sensual appeal.

He was just a tougher version of that charming rogue Nigel Browning, she told herself fiercely. She mustn't forget what a long time it had taken for that grievous wound to heal. In fact, she wasn't even sure that she *had* totally recovered either confidence in herself as a woman, or in her judgement of other people.

So, she had made the right decision—hadn't she? What else could she have done but to take rapid evasive action as far as Luke was concerned? Despite the fact that she still had great difficulty in sleeping at night, and, if she was to be honest, longed for him with every fibre of her being, Angelica knew that she wouldn't be able to survive another romantic catastrophe such as she'd suffered over her betrayal at Nigel's hands.

The arrival of a laughing, noisy group of people crowding into the small gallery interrupted her troubled thoughts. Realising that it was about time she left, Angelica rose to her feet, crossing the upper hall and descending the main staircase. Just as she was deciding to take one last look at the amazing tiles and decoration in the Arab Hall, she'd barely taken one step forward—before she suddenly froze in fright.

It couldn't possibly be…? Could it…? And then, as she blinked, she had no doubt that it really *was* Luke Cunningham's tall, commanding figure making his way through the crowd of people towards her.

With a gasp of horror, she hurriedly ducked back behind an enormous copper urn filled with a shimmering display of brilliant peacock feathers. Closing her eyes and clutching her glass tightly to her chest, she prayed with every fibre of her being that she had moved swiftly enough to avoid detection. Hidden here, within a dark enclave beneath the stairs, and shielded by the giant urn, she might just be safe. She had no idea why Luke was at this party to launch the exhibition, but he surely wouldn't have expected to find her here, would he?

A moment later, she realised that her fervent prayers and hopes had all been in vain.

'There you are! I've been looking for you everywhere,' the deep voice drawled, and she cautiously and warily opened her eyes to see his tall, dark figure looming over her.

'Come on—the party's breaking up now,' he added, removing the glass from her trembling fingers as she continued to stare silently up at him with confused, dazed eyes. 'It's time for us to go.'

'Go? Go where . . . ?' she gasped, her brain in a whirl as he quickly grasped hold of her arm, whisking her through a small door hidden behind the staircase, and down a long, dark passage. 'What do you think you're doing? You can't k-kidnap me like this!'

Luke laughed. 'As I think I've said to you before now, it seems that I can—and I have!' he drawled, still keeping a firm grip on her dazed figure as he opened a large door, pulling her after him into a quiet, tree-lined road running alongside Leighton House.

With hardly time to catch her breath, Angelica found herself being swiftly towed across the pavement, to where a chauffeur was holding open the door of a long black limousine. And then she was being bundled into the back seat, before being joined by Luke.

'OK, Colin. You know where to go,' Luke told the chauffeur, before firmly closing the glass screen between the driver and the large passenger compartment, and settling himself back down on the soft leather seat beside her.

'You can't *do* this! I demand to know——'

'Why don't you shut up, Angelica?' Luke's hard, firm voice cut briskly across her breathless protest. 'First of all, you must know that I am very far from being a kidnapper!' He gave a snort of wry, sardonic laughter. 'I am, in fact, merely intending to take you out to dinner. However, if it makes you feel any better, I will happily give you my word of honour that you are quite safe, that I have absolutely no intention of laying a finger on you. So why don't you just sit back and enjoy the ride?'

CHAPTER SIX

HER mind in a whirl, Angelica allowed herself to be led across the thick carpeting towards a table in a quiet corner of the vast dining-room.

'I'll never forgive you for this!' she hissed at Luke, through teeth clenched in a false, stiff smile. 'On top of everything else, I'm not even wearing the right clothes, for heaven's sake!'

'Nonsense,' he murmured, glancing down at her slender, supple body in the straight aquamarine chiffon dress, a pale green and aquamarine sequinned scarf clasped around her slim hips. 'You look wonderful—like a beautiful sea nymph or mermaid.'

If it hadn't been such a public place, and if she hadn't been surrounded by so many witnesses, Angelica would cheerfully have kicked the awful man in the shins.

It had seemed such an amusing idea, earlier this evening, to attend the art exhibition in a 1920s costume taken from her grandmother's hamper of theatrical clothes. But it was definitely *not* funny to find herself now wearing such a ridiculous dress—to dine at the Ritz, of all places!

'Why did you have to drag me here?' she muttered angrily as a waiter held out a chair for her.

Luke didn't immediately reply, waiting while large linen napkins were placed on their laps with a flourish, and their glasses filled from a large bottle of champagne already cooling in its silver ice bucket beside the table.

'I can think of some worse fates in life than dining here,' he said at last with a sardonic grin. 'Besides, there are several reasons why I decided that this was the perfect venue. In the first place, it's generally agreed that the Ritz hotel has one of the prettiest dining-rooms in London. Secondly, as you can see, this is a very well-lit public place, where I knew that you would feel entirely safe.' He shrugged. 'But there is nothing to stop you getting up and walking out of here, if you wish to do so. Although, of course, I very much hope that you won't.'

Angelica glared at him for a moment, before staring down at the snowy white linen tablecloth.

Who was he kidding? Luke must know that she wasn't the sort of person who enjoyed making scenes in public. So it looked as though he'd got her over a barrel for the moment, she thought with glum resignation, before slowly raising her head to gaze at her surroundings.

Angelica had to agree that he was right about one thing, at least. The large dining-room was certainly quite one of the most beautifully decorated rooms that she'd ever seen. Designed in a French rococo style, the walls and ornate plasterwork covered in soft tones of apricot, blue, pink and gold, it really was an enchanting sight. And, since she was hungry, and seldom, if ever had the opportunity to dine in such wildly expensive, luxurious surroundings, maybe she might as well make the most of it? Or just for a little while, anyway, she quickly assured herself.

Silently sipping her champagne, she glanced through her eyelashes at Luke. He and the head waiter were discussing the menu which, like the champagne, he had apparently already ordered in advance. And wasn't that just typical of his usual totally arrogant assumption that he would always get his own way? she told herself grimly.

It might be Dutch courage, but the heady effect of yet more alcohol—in addition to the amount she'd already consumed at the exhibition—was definitely beginning to make her feel a whole lot better. It was clearly about time that Luke realised he couldn't keep on pushing her around.

'So, OK, it's a beautiful room, and I'm enjoying this champagne,' she said, deliberately keeping her tone of voice cool and detached. 'And, since I *can* leave any time I wish to, maybe you'd care to tell me why I should stay?'

Luke leaned back in his chair, regarding her with an amused grin. 'That's what I love about you, Angelica—you may be down, but you're never out for the count. I might have known that you'd soon be up off the canvas and slugging away at me again—as usual!'

'You certainly deserve a good punch on the nose,' she agreed with grim relish. 'However, I'm still waiting to hear exactly *why* you've brought me here?'

'Ah, yes...' He paused for a moment, slowly revolving the slim glass stem of his champagne flute, as if buried deep in thought. 'One of the things on which I think we can agree is that we first met in very unusual circumstances,' he said at last.

'You can say that again!' she agreed waspishly.

'And once having got off on the wrong foot, so to speak, our subsequent encounters, while—er—interesting, having not given us an opportunity really to get to know one another.'

'But you've seen my house. And, after inviting yourself into my kitchen, you also know a lot about the problems I've been facing. So what else could you want to know about me?' she asked belligerently.

Luke shrugged his broad shoulders. 'Yes, I may know something about your surroundings and way of life—but I know nothing about your past, your education, what books you like to read, or your favourite type of music, for instance. And, of course, you know absolutely nothing about me either.'

'And if I said that I really didn't want to know anything about you...?' she replied quickly, determined not to let this man ride roughshod over her yet again.

'You could say it—but you wouldn't be telling the truth.'

'My God, you're arrogant!' she ground out savagely, her cheeks flaming under the steady gaze of his hooded grey eyes.

Unfortunately she was prevented from saying any more by the arrival of a waiter, bearing their first course of Parma ham with melon.

After the waiter had eventually left them alone, there was a long silence before Luke reached out to clasp hold of her nervously trembling hand.

'I want you to listen to me for a moment, Angelica.' His voice was steely, the hard note of serious intent reflected in the stern expression on his face.

'There is absolutely no point in playing games with one another. In fact, it's a complete waste of time. And trying to pretend that there isn't a very strong sexual attraction between us is equally futile. However,' he added firmly as she opened her mouth to protest, 'we are both grown-up, sensible people. We know that this type of impulsive, wild infatuation can be dangerous. And that even the most sensible people can get badly hurt and wounded. So I am merely trying to place our relationship—for want of another word—on a more normal basis.'

He paused, but when she remained silent he continued, 'I'm sorry if I seem to have taken matters rather forcefully into my own hands tonight. But I would like us to try and begin again. I want you, if you can, to imagine that we hardly know one another, that I have asked you out to dinner simply for the enjoyment of your company, and what might be—who knows?—the start of a long and enduring friendship. But above all, my dear Angelica, I want you to relax and learn to trust me.' He gave her a warm and engaging smile. 'To realise that I have no intention of harming even one hair on your beautiful head.'

'That's—er—quite a speech,' she muttered, impressed despite herself by the tone of deep sincerity in his voice. Unfortunately, with his close proximity, and so much alcohol now flowing through her veins, she was finding it difficult to think clearly. Once again, the arguments seemed to be violently see-sawing back and forth in her confused brain.

He'd asked for her trust, but that wasn't something that could be just handed to someone on a plate. Trust and confidence took time, and had to be earned. Besides, as she knew to her cost, even the most trustworthy-seeming people could and did let you down.

But surely there wouldn't be any harm in just enjoying a meal with him? After all, it wasn't likely that she'd ever have the opportunity to dine in such style again, certainly not in the foreseeable future.

On the other hand, there was no denying the sleepless nights and tortured dreams which could be laid at the door of this man's dark attraction, nor the fact that she was almost insanely drawn to his overwhelmingly masculine, sensual appeal. So it would be total folly to remain in his company one moment longer than necessary.

Despite knowing that she was probably being a complete and utter fool, Angelica took a deep breath and proceeded to throw both her hat—and her heart—over a windmill.

'While I have severe doubts about "a long and enduring friendship", I suppose I may as well stick around,' she murmured, her cheeks flushing as she realised her hand was still firmly in the grip of his warm fingers.

'Does that mean that you've decided to have dinner with me?'

She nodded, withdrawing her hand from his. 'Although I can't help thinking it will be a miracle if we get through even this first course without coming to blows,' she told him with a wry laugh.

'That's a great deal better,' he grinned. 'I've hardly ever seen you smile.'

'I haven't had a great deal to laugh or smile about lately,' she said, before quickly deciding to change the subject, since any reference to their past encounters might not be a good idea. 'If you're going to relate your life story, don't you think you'd better start fairly soon? Otherwise we might be here all night.'

He laughed. 'I can promise you that it's not going to take that long! In fact, I can give you the salient points very quickly.'

However, as the meal progressed, and she listened to him relating the story of his boyhood, Angelica realised that he'd had very much the same warm and happy, if fairly solitary upbringing that she herself had experienced.

Having grown up in the United States—his mother had divorced his father when he was very young, and married his American stepfather shortly afterwards—Luke wryly confessed to being fairly wild when young. 'I guess I more or less fooled my way through college, passing the exams more by luck than hard work!' he grinned. However, it seemed that he'd settled down to doing a Master's degree in business studies at Harvard, before returning to England, on the death of his father, to take over the family's ailing engineering company in the Midlands.

'Yes,' he agreed when she pressed him on the subject. 'It took a lot of hard work to eventually make the firm profitable. In fact, it's probably fair to say that for the last fifteen years I've been what could be termed a workaholic.'

'But where does the bank come into all this? It doesn't sound to me as though you're really such a "lowly worm" after all,' she teased.

'Well, to be honest—and we are being honest tonight, aren't we?—I suppose that I ought to confess that I do now own a private merchant bank, as well as many other companies.'

'Goodness!' She blinked in surprise. 'From what you say, it sounds as though you're definitely a big cheese in the business world.'

He threw back his dark head and roared with laughter, the sound drawing the attention of the other diners at the tables near by.

'Oh, Angelica—you really are priceless!' His broad shoulders shook with amusement. 'No one has ever called me that before, although I suppose it is just marginally more flattering than "sunshine"! But, yes, I suppose I have been reasonably successful.'

As the evening wore on, they were so immersed in talking and discovering one another's likes and dislikes that it was a shock to Angelica to discover that she had, somehow, managed to consume a delicious meal of salmon with hollandaise sauce, fillet of lamb with leek and fennel, and iced pear *sabayon*, without almost any recollection of having done so!

However, by the time coffee was being served, the atmosphere between them seemed subtly to alter and change. Despite their light and easy conversation, she became gripped by a feeling of strain and tension. A breathless, feverish sensation, in which she was vividly aware of even the slightest movement of Luke's powerful body, sharply conscious of the shadows thrown by the soft lighting on his high cheekbones, and of a pulse beating strongly in his hard, firm jaw.

'I think it's time I took you home,' he said suddenly, and her eyes flew to his as she registered the harsh note of constraint in his voice. 'I did, after all, give you my word of honour that I wouldn't lay a finger on you.'

'Yes, so you did,' she agreed quietly.

'On the other hand——' he paused for a split-second '—we could always continue this conversation over another cup of coffee—at my apartment. I live virtually around the corner, within easy walking distance of this hotel.'

The air between them was palpably full of tension. And then Angelica was astonished to hear herself saying, 'Yes, I . . . I think I'd like that.'

He gazed into the luminous blue eyes, noting the hectic flush on her cheeks and the barely perceptible, nervous tremor of her soft lips.

'I don't want there to be any misunderstanding, Angelica,' he said softly, once more placing his warm hand over her fingers. 'I don't make any guarantees for the future. But tonight I gave you my word—so this is a genuine, straight invitation for coffee. OK?'

She nodded quickly, astonished to find that she wasn't sure whether to be glad or sorry to hear that Luke wasn't intending to seduce her. It could only be the amount of alcohol she'd consumed, she told herself sternly, knowing that she ought to be thoroughly ashamed of even a moment's sharp pang of regret.

'Shall we go?' he murmured, putting down his napkin and helping her up from her seat.

As they walked slowly out of the restaurant, Angelica realised that her guardian angel must have been working overtime on her behalf. Because, if she had given in to that crazy, feverish desire to be seduced by this man, the outcome could only have been disastrous.

A sophisticated, worldly man like Luke—who must have slept with hundreds of women—would only have been bored and irritated by her lack of expertise. Her only experiment with lovemaking had been with Nigel, and the whole business had been such a fiasco that she'd never had any wish to repeat the experience. So she probably should thank her lucky stars, and be grateful that she'd been spared the humiliation resulting from any deeper involvement with Luke.

Immersed in her thoughts, Angelica was sharply jerked back to reality by a high-pitched voice, hailing Luke across the wide expanse of the foyer.

'*Darling*! What on earth are you doing here?'

A moment later a beautifully dressed, slim, dark-haired woman was smiling up at him, before confidently raising her lovely face for his kiss.

'Mmm...darling, how lovely to see you. I had no idea you'd be here tonight. It's Aunt Doreen's birthday—and we've been having a little private party. You really should have come and joined us.'

The dark woman's voice was extraordinarily musical, only sharpening slightly as she turned her large dark eyes on his companion.

'I don't think we've met before...?'

'No, Eleanor, I don't think you have,' Luke agreed blandly, before formally introducing them to each other.

Angelica barely registered the other woman's name. She was desperately trying to cope with a totally irrational, deeply instinctive feeling of sharp dislike for someone who was, after all, a complete stranger.

'Er—how do you do?' she muttered, almost quailing as the woman—who was wearing a crimson silk outfit which could only have come from a French couturier—raised a delicately arched dark eyebrow as her gaze ran swiftly over Angelica.

'An original twenties dress? How quaint!' Eleanor murmured, before turning back to Luke. 'Darling, do come and meet Aunt Doreen. I've told her so much about us that I know she'd love to see you.'

'Well, I'm afraid that we're just on our way out...' Luke began, when the dark-haired woman gave a peal of laughter.'

'Relax, darling—we're leaving as well. So *please* just come over and wish the old dear a happy birthday,' Eleanor begged, tugging impatiently at his arm.

Luke shrugged and turned to smile at Angelica, before taking her hand and towing her reluctant figure after him as he followed the other girl across the pink-carpeted foyer, with its marble columns and sparkling mirrors, towards a small group of elderly men and women.

'Look who I've brought over to see you!' Eleanor exclaimed happily to an old woman standing in the middle of the group. 'You've heard all about my friendship with Luke Cunningham, of course.'

'Ah, yes—how nice to see you at last.' The elderly lady gave him a brief smile, offering a limp hand heavily encrusted with diamond rings. 'I understand that you're a very successful financier?'

Luke's dark brows came together in a quick frown. But he was given no opportunity to say anything in reply, as she continued in an imperious voice, 'In which case, I sincerely hope that you're soon going to make an honest woman of my niece? I don't at all approve of the way young people carry on these days.'

'Oh, Aunt Doreen—for heaven's sake!' Eleanor exclaimed with a happy, confident laugh. 'Give the poor man a chance! I'm sure that we'll both settle down together when we're good and ready to do so.'

The 'poor man' had stiffened during this exchange, his expression hardening into a blank, inscrutable mask. But Angelica had no eyes for Luke. She was staring with a horrified gaze at Eleanor's Aunt Doreen. Oh, no! Surely it couldn't *really* be awful old Lady Marshall...?

Unfortunately, it was.

As their eyes met, Lady Marshall's expression of shock and stunned disbelief almost matched Angelica's.

'Who, may I ask, had both the impertinence and effrontery to bring *that girl* here?'

As the imperious tones rang out in the foyer, everyone turned to view Angelica's trembling figure.

'Miss Lonsdale has been my guest at dinner.' Luke's deep voice rose above the hubbub of

Eleanor's startled questions, and her aunt's explanation of her role as chairman of the Lonsdale Trust.

'Well! I hope you've been explaining to this young girl that money doesn't grow on trees,' Lady Marshall told Luke. 'It's my opinion that she's sadly lacking in any financial sense. However, dear Eleanor is intending to go over the accounts of Lonsdale House. I'm sure she'll be able to make considerable savings all round. Take that old housekeeper, for instance. She's quite hopeless. The sooner she's given the sack the better!'

'*What* . . .? Over my dead body! Betty's worth a hundred times more than you . . . you stupid old trout!' Angelica cried, finding her voice at last. 'Betty worked her fingers to the bone for my grandmother, both in the theatre and later at Lonsdale House. And what have you ever done?' she demanded furiously. 'Nothing but flash your skinny legs in the chorus and . . . and bamboozle a dotty old man into making you Lady Marshall—instead of plain Doreen Summers from East Ham!'

'Calm down, Angelica . . .'

'Take your rotten hands off me!' she yelled at Luke, who had gripped hold of her arm. 'You're just as bad as that wicked old woman—worse, in fact. Because you're nothing but an evil snake in the grass! Chatting me up, just so you could tell your precious Eleanor how badly I've arranged Sir T-Tristram's c-collection!'

'That's absolute nonsense!' he growled.

But Angelica was too wound up to listen. 'Sneaking your way into my house under false pretences!' she wailed. 'How...how *could* you do such an awful thing...?'

A moment later she'd wriggled out of his grasp and taken to her heels, tears streaming down her face as she ran full pelt down the long foyer towards the main entrance of the hotel.

Angelica picked up the telephone, only listening to the voice on the other end for a moment before slamming it sharply down again.

'Who was that, dear?' Betty asked, busily engaged in rolling out some pastry.

'No one of any importance,' Angelica told her grimly. 'Just that rat-fink, still trying to weasel his way back into this house.'

'Don't you think that you ought to give him a chance to explain?' the older woman murmured, despite knowing that she was wasting her breath.

'Explain what?' Angelica asked wearily. 'How many times do I have to tell you that he's in league with all the rest of them? In fact, Luke Cunningham is just like Nigel Browning!'

'I really don't think——'

'Oh, yes, he is,' Angelica ground out. 'Charming his way into this house, munching his oily way through your home-made jam and cake, just so he could report back to old Lady Marshall, and that awful Eleanor. Have I told you that they were clearly having an affair? And that he's planning to marry her?'

Betty sighed heavily. 'Yes, dear, you have. Several times.'

'Well, there you are, then.'

'I wish I did know where we are.' Betty sighed again. 'Because I'm sure that you're wrong. I can't believe that nice Mr Cunningham had any interest in anything other than getting to know you. Really smitten, I thought he was, and that's a fact.'

'Ha! That's a laugh,' Angelica muttered grimly as she left the kitchen.

Only, of course, she had absolutely nothing to laugh about. Ever since that horrendous scene in the foyer of the Ritz hotel, just over a week ago, she'd barely been able to believe what had happened to her. How could she have had such appalling luck as to meet two charming rogues—and to have been taken in so easily by both of them?

It was a question which dominated her mind during the day, and haunted her virtually sleepless nights. And despite the almost constant phone calls from Luke, and his attempt to gain entrance to Lonsdale House, she had adamantly refused to see him.

Avoiding any contact with him on the day that the house was open had proved to be a problem, of course. Until she'd had the brainwave of asking her old friend, Kim, to stand in for her. Freshly back from swinging New York, Kim had willingly agreed to help out, and Angelica would have been more grateful if her friend hadn't also fallen under the awful man's spell.

'But he's gorgeous!' she'd exclaimed when Angelica had returned—via the back entrance to the garden—after all the visitors had left. 'And he wasn't best pleased to find that you'd flown the coop,' Kim had added with a worried frown. 'I honestly don't think that he's the sort of man to play games with. He struck me as very determined and, although it probably sounds mad to say so, very dangerous!'

'Rubbish!' Angelica had snorted irritably. 'I just couldn't face a row with him, that's all. He'll get fed up and leave me alone very soon. You'll see.'

Kim had shrugged. 'Well, I hope for your sake that you're right. Mind you, he can leave his shoes outside *my* bedroom door any night! I bet he's a real tiger in bed!'

'Don't be so disgusting!' Angelica had retorted grimly, wondering why her friendship with Kim had lasted as long as it had.

However, far more important than Luke Cunningham—or his attempts to contact her—was the worrying situation over Lonsdale House and its board of trustees. Or, to be strictly accurate, the attitude of the chairman, Lady Marshall.

Angelica didn't need anyone to tell her that she now must have a very real enemy in the autocratic old lady. Not that she wouldn't firmly stand by everything she'd said in Betty's defence that evening at the Ritz, of course. And repeat it again, if necessary. However, it didn't take a very high IQ to realise that the venomous old dragon would now be after her blood—or that if she could turf Angelica out of Lonsdale House she'd have considerable pleasure doing so.

Unfortunately, there had been a deathly silence so far, which Angelica found extremely worrying. And it was a problem which was made even more unsettling by the fact that it was one she couldn't discuss with Betty, since she had no intention of allowing her old nanny to be distressed or upset in any way.

So, when Betty had nagged her to see to the old mulberry tree, which had been damaged in that fierce rainstorm some weeks ago, she'd been quite pleased to have something positive to do. Even if she *was* frightened of heights, this was hardly a seven-storey job, she told herself firmly as she dragged the old wooden ladder out of the garden shed. Placing it up against the ancient tree, whose broken branches needed trimming, she picked up a heavy saw and began gingerly climbing up the rungs.

This old mulberry tree, with its sharp-tasting crimson berries—which Betty made into the most delicious fruit pies—had supposedly been one of many planted in the garden of Henry VIII's old manor house at Chelsea almost five hundred years ago. Angelica realised that it was probably just a fable, but some other gardens in Cheyne Walk contained trees equally old, just as their garden walls— like Lonsdale House—had been partly built with bricks and stone fragments from the King's manor house, when it was demolished early in the eighteenth century.

So, whether the story was true or not, Angelica always took great care to look after their old mulberry tree as carefully as possible. However, she was only too well aware that she wasn't a dab hand with a saw. How did carpenters always make it look so easy? They never seemed to get the damn thing stuck halfway through a branch, as she had at the moment, she told herself grimly, swearing out loud as she wrestled with the saw, which was obstinately refusing to be either pushed or pulled free of the wood.

'I am deeply shocked to hear a nicely brought-up girl using such disgraceful language! Whoa... *careful*!'

Angelica, who'd shrieked and jumped in fright at the sound of that familiar deep voice, was too busy trying to cling on to the old wooden ladder to have time to enquire exactly how Luke had managed to gain access to the garden. Creaking and groaning, the ladder swayed perilously back and forth between the branches.

'Hold on, I'll be right with you,' he called out, beginning to climb up to her rescue.

'What do you *think* I'm d-doing?' she gasped, clamping her eyes tightly shut, her hands frozen in terror on the top rung. 'P-please hurry up—and get me out of here!'

A moment later, as he stood on the rung beneath her feet, she could feel the hard warmth of his body against her back.

'It's all right, darling. Relax—lean back against me. You'll be quite safe,' he murmured, reaching up to ease her rigid fingers gently off the rung.

'If... if you hadn't appeared out of n-nowhere, and given me such a f-fright,' she stuttered angrily, 'I'd never have.... *Aggh*!'

Later, when she had both the time and the opportunity to work out what had happened, Angelica realised that some of the rungs on the old ladder were none too safe. And Luke's weight had proved to be the final straw. However, all she knew at the time was that they were both slipping swiftly downwards, as though in an express elevator, with Luke's arms clasped tightly about her.

Dazed and shocked, Angelica was astonished on landing to find herself standing upright, and in one piece. As Luke carefully turned her around, she slumped helplessly against his broad chest, her legs feeling as if they'd suddenly been turned to jelly, and her knees knocking together like castanets.

'You damn little fool!' he rasped, almost shaking her inert form as he was seized by a sudden storm of anger. 'If I hadn't been here, God knows what would have happened! Don't you realise that you could have been killed?'

And then he was kissing her roughly, without a shred of tenderness, as though the sheer ferocity of his cruel lips and harshly invasive tongue could somehow expunge his fear for her safety.

And Angelica, too, found herself caught up in the feverish, passionate force of his hard anger and fury. As always, when she found herself in this man's arms, it felt as though she'd been set on fire, a flame roaring through her mind and trembling body, consuming all resistance and leaving only the driving need to yield in a molten mass of over-whelming need and desire.

She was being swept away on a tidal wave of pure pleasure, her whole world encompassed by the pressure of his lips on hers, the hard strength of his arms about her trembling figure. Mindless with passionate desire, she frantically arched her body against him, sharply aware of his hard arousal and the blinding revelation that she wanted nothing more than to yield—to surrender completely to the overwhelming, driving force inside her clamouring for release.

'I'm not going to apologise for that kiss.' His voice was ragged as he slowly raised his head. 'It's only a fraction of what you deserve for giving me such a hard time this week. Surely, Angelica,' he added savagely, 'you must have *known* that I'd track you down sooner or later?'

'Yes, I...I suppose I did,' she muttered, her words muffled as she buried her face in his shoulder, still trying to come to terms with the revelation of her deep feelings for this man, a man who had not only betrayed her, but who was also heavily involved with another woman.

'Then why do you keep on running away?' he demanded harshly, leading her trembling figure over to a bench in a sunny corner of the garden.

'Why do you think?' she murmured, closing her eyes for a moment as she raised her face to the warm rays of the afternoon sun. 'And how *did* you know I'd be out here in the garden this afternoon?' she added wearily, before answering her own question. 'It was Betty, wasn't it?'

'Yes,' he replied bluntly. 'At least she has some sense in her head, which is more than I can say for you!'

'So, now you've found me, what *do* you want, Luke? A quick look at the accounts?' she queried bitterly.

'Don't be so damn stupid!' he ground out through clenched teeth. 'I couldn't care less about your accounts—or only in so far as they worry and upset you.'

'Well, in that case, why *are* you here?'

'Because, having given the matter some considerable thought, I now see that the solution to all our problems is for you and me to get married.'

CHAPTER SEVEN

ANGELICA stared at him in open-mouthed astonishment for some moments.

'*What*...?' she gasped finally. 'What did you just
say?'

'It's really very simple,' Luke told her coolly, the
anger over her narrow escape from injury slowly
draining out of his long, tall body as he leaned
casually back on the bench. 'I'm suggesting that
we should get married.'

'B-but...b-but why?' she stammered, her mind
in a complete daze.

'Why not?' he drawled calmly. 'I would have
thought it made perfect sense.'

'You do...?'

'Certainly. And, after that quite extraordinary
outburst of yours in the Ritz hotel, it's obvious that
a marriage between us will be the perfect solution
to both our problems.'

Angelica shook her head in distraction, convinced that she must have a screw loose somewhere
in her brain. Not only did she have absolutely no
idea of what he was talking about, but it felt as if
she was listening to the answer to a riddle, without
first having heard the question.

'Look...I'm sorry to be so dim, but could we
go back to the beginning?' she asked him plaintively, brushing a distracted hand through her long,
pale hair. 'I don't know anything about what

124

problems *you* may have—I've been too busy worrying about my own.'

He gave a caustic laugh. 'I'm not surprised—especially with Lady Marshall on the war-path!'

'All right! There's no need for you to rub it in,' she muttered glumly. 'I know I shouldn't have been so rude to the beastly old woman—not that I didn't mean what I said, because I most definitely did!' she added defiantly. 'However, I do realise that I behaved very badly.'

'Alas, I'm afraid you did,' he murmured, his lips twitching with amusement. 'Lady Marshall's shrieks of rage, before collapsing into a state of complete hysterics, was a scene I'm not likely to forget in a hurry!'

'OK, OK!' She glowered at him. 'But if you expect me to apologise to you...'

'Apologise to *me*?' He lifted a dark quizzical eyebrow. 'Whatever for? Quite frankly, I haven't seen anything so funny for a very long time!'

As he gave a sharp bark of sardonic laughter, Angelica closed her eyes for a moment. Was it possible that, in some mysterious way, she'd damaged her brain during that rapid slide down the ladder just now? Because surely Luke ought to be furious at the way she'd treated his girlfriend's aunt?

'I'm sorry, but I really don't understand...' She shook her head helplessly. 'Can you *please* explain—and as simply as possible—exactly what's going on? I mean... why this sudden proposal of marriage? Especially when it seemed fairly obvious the other night that your girlfriend is clearly expecting you to marry her,' she added waspishly.

His features hardened to a chilly mask, but he merely shrugged before drawling coolly, 'If I had ever considered the idea of marrying Eleanor Nicholson, I can assure you that I no long have any intention of doing so. Therefore there is no need for you to be worried, or——'

'Me? Worried? Do me a favour, *sunshine*!' Angelica gave a shrill, high-pitched laugh. 'I couldn't care less about your relationship with that awful woman—or her ghastly aunt. As far as I'm concerned, you're more than welcome to them both. But if you think I'm going to marry you, just so they can get their feet in the door, here at Lonsdale House, you're very much mistaken!'

'Don't be so damned silly!' he growled. 'There's absolutely *no* question of my either betraying you, or of being in collusion with Lady Marshall.'

'But... but I thought...'

'For heaven's sake, Angelica! Surely you must have realised that I'd never even met the old woman until after her birthday party at the Ritz. Haven't you been listening to a word I've said?'

'Yes, I have,' she retorted. 'But none of it seems to make any sense. If you're *not* involved with Lady Marshall, what on earth are you doing here?'

'May the good Lord give me strength!' he ground out impatiently, brushing a hand roughly through his thick, dark hair. 'It's precisely *because* you badly need help in coping with the old harpy, as well as all your other problems, that a marriage between us makes perfect sense.'

'It may be sense to you, but it sounds more like double Dutch to me,' she sighed. 'How about trying to keep this all very simple? Leaving my problems aside for the moment, why don't you tell me about *your* reasons for wanting to get married?'

He regarded her from beneath his heavy eyelids in silence for some moments, before giving a shrug of his broad shoulders.

'To put it very simply, I feel that I'm at a crossroads in my life,' he began slowly. 'Like many men in my position, there comes a time when you begin to realise that there's a great deal more to life than the pursuit of money or success. Which is not to say that I haven't enjoyed building up my own particular financial empire—because I have. However, I am now a very wealthy man, and I'm looking for some other worlds to conquer—or, possibly, just to enjoy doing something completely different with my life!'

'Hold it!' she demanded suddenly. 'How old are you?'

He frowned. 'Thirty-six. Although I can't see what my age has to do with it.'

'Well, aren't you a bit young to be suffering from a mid-life crisis?' she asked caustically. 'And, if you're trying to convince me that you're really a sweet little pussy cat, forget it! Anyone further from being a SNAG would be hard to find.'

'What on earth are you talking about?'

She sighed and rolled her eyes up at the sky. 'If you don't know that SNAG stands for Sensitive New Age Guy, maybe you really *do* have one foot in the grave, after all?'

'Thank you for those few kind words,' he snapped, his mouth tightening into a hard line as she gave him a malicious grin. 'And I am definitely *not* a nice little pussy cat!'

'No, you certainly aren't!' she agreed with feeling, adding quickly as his dark brows flew together in an angry frown, 'OK, I'm sorry...'

'Someone is going to wring your neck one of these days, Angelica,' he grated. 'And believe me you'll deserve it! However, *if* I may continue...?' he added silkily, a decidedly dangerous note of menace in his voice.

'Er...yes, of course—er—carry on,' she mumbled quickly.

'I was merely pointing out that I've been beginning to look at my way of life, and asking myself some pertinent questions. Such as: do I want to continue living in a huge, glamorous but definitely soulless penthouse apartment in Mayfair? And, while an address book full of the names of beautiful women is all very well, isn't it time that I settled down with a wife and children? Also, is there really any point in continuing to amass money for its own sake? Should I put my talents to some better use— such as helping to organise and raise money for charities, for instance?'

'Now, that really *is* a good idea.' Angelica nodded with approval. 'There are so many worthwhile causes just crying out for some help with their funds.'

'I'm glad you approve,' he murmured drily.

'I'm not sure that I approve of your overflowing address book. But I assume that *dear* Eleanor is in there somewhere, among your female hit-list?'

'It would be extremely ungentlemanly of me to say anything about Eleanor Nicholson,' he retorted curtly. 'Except to mention that she's a very clever and successful accountant who will undoubtedly make some lucky man a wonderful wife.'

'I was under the impression, from what I saw at the Ritz, that you were all lined up to be the lucky man...' she murmured caustically.

'I've already stated my position as far as Eleanor is concerned,' he told her firmly. 'However, I can give you my solemn word that I had never met her aunt before I was introduced to her at the Ritz hotel.'

'Well, I can tell you that Lady Marshall is a thoroughly nasty, evil woman!' Angelica exclaimed heatedly. 'Did you hear what she said about poor Betty?'

'Yes, of course I did—just as everyone certainly heard your reply!' He gave a bark of laughter. 'However, I agree that Lady Marshall is to be avoided like the plague. I had no idea she was the chairman of your trustees, but I can easily understand your problems in trying to deal with the old bat!'

'Well...! It's beginning to look as if I may have misjudged you, Luke,' she told him with a wide grin. 'Maybe you really aren't so bad after all!'

'Thank you,' he laughed.

'However, although the whole idea is completely ridiculous, of course, I completely fail to see—even if you're bored to sobs with your way of life—why you should want to marry me.'

'I would have thought it was obvious,' he shrugged. 'Let's look at your set-up. You have a part-time job as a tourist guide, but it only brings in a few pounds a week—certainly not enough to live on. You have inherited half of this charming house, with its weird and crazy museum, but you can't sell it. Nor, at the same time, can you afford to keep it in good condition. In fact, it hangs like an albatross around your neck. And, just to compound your problems, you have a board of trustees whose chairman is obviously quite impossible to deal with.'

'You can say that again!'

'So it's obvious that you need a large injection of money, both to maintain the fabric of the house and also to employ a first-rate curator to rearrange and run the museum. Spending a sum on advertising Sir Tristram's collection would also be a good idea, and certainly bring many more people to the house.'

'But I——'

'Hang on a minute—I haven't finished,' he told her briskly. 'I do also have a private, personal reason for being concerned with both you and this house. Unfortunately, I can't discuss it at the moment. Mainly because I could be wrong, and the fact that I'm still awaiting confirmation from my lawyers in America.

'However, leaving that aside,' he continued quickly as she frowned at him in puzzlement, 'I don't think you should underestimate the problem of Lady Marshall. I will lay any odds you like that by telling her a few home truths the other night you've definitely cooked your goose as far as she's concerned. Although I enjoyed your spirited defence, of both yourself and Betty, I'm quite sure that she will have been in touch with her lawyers to see if she has any way of evicting you from this house.'

'Yes.' Angelica sighed heavily. 'I expect that you're right. I don't think she can actually get rid of me—but that won't stop her trying, will it?'

Luke shook his dark head. 'I'm afraid not. Which is why you need a white knight to come galloping to your rescue. One who is not only extremely rich, but also used to the hard, tough infighting of the business scene, and not worried about taking on the Lady Marshalls of this world. And, therefore, while it may be immodest of me to say so, I think I fill the bill admirably!'

There was a long silence, before Angelica slowly rose to her feet and began pacing up and down the lawn in front of the bench.

'I'm not sure if I've got this right,' she said at last, turning to face him, 'but it sounds as if you are offering to marry me because you're fed up with your present way of life, don't much care for your luxurious apartment, and want to avoid marrying a determined woman—with whom you're having an affair...'

'No—you're wrong,' he interjected quickly. 'I haven't—er—had anything to do with Eleanor for some time. Not since first meeting you, in fact.'

'Oh, wow! Am I supposed to be flattered by that fact?' Angelica enquired sweetly through clenched teeth.

He shrugged. 'I was merely putting the record straight,' he told her coolly. 'However, it occurs to me that I should maybe state, at this point in our discussion, that I firmly believe in the sanctity of marriage. Which means that I would expect both of us to be entirely faithful to one another.'

'Wow—you really *are* intending to change the habits of a lifetime, aren't you?' she retorted sarcastically. 'So, it appears that in return for rescuing you from a boring apartment, a tedious job and Eleanor—who is clearly a number-crunching, predatory female—you are offering to spend thousands of pounds putting this house and Sir Tristram's collection in good condition. Right?'

'Correct. *And* I'm guaranteeing to get Lady Marshall off your back,' he reminded her with a sardonic grin. 'That alone must be worth a fortune!'

'Yes—if I were interested solely in money. But, while I've been listening carefully to all that garbage you've been spouting about finance and marriage, I've yet to hear why you want to marry *me*. You could, after all, solve all your problems at one stroke by picking any one of the names from your large address book. *And* save yourself a fortune at the same time. So why me, of all people?'

'Because you're bright, amusing and you'd never be boring,' he answered promptly. 'Because I would enjoy being able to look after you, and to ensure that you have a comfortable lifestyle—it might be fun to have a place in the country for weekends, for instance. And, of course, there's Betty,' he added with a grin. 'By marrying you, I can make sure of an endless supply of home-made jam and chocolate cake!'

'Is that all?' she demanded stonily.

'Of course not.' He gave a low, sensual laugh as he rose to his feet and began walking towards her. 'In fact, my dear Angelica, you know very well that it isn't!'

'I...I don't know anything of the sort,' she muttered, backing hurriedly away from his advancing figure, her progress interrupted as she bumped into a nearby oak tree.

'Oh, yes, you do!' he taunted with a cruel, sardonic smile as he moved slowly, like a leopard stalking his prey, and she found herself trapped with her back hard up against the rough bark of the tree.

'Get lost!' she gasped. 'If you think that I'm for sale, or that I can be taken over like...like some of those companies you now control, you're dead wrong!'

'Ah—but I'm dead right about this...!' he said huskily, putting his hands firmly about her waist and pulling her closely to him. 'You may be a totally maddening girl, who regularly drives me up the wall, but...but when you're in my arms there's an undeniable spark of magic between us.'

'No!' she gasped helplessly as he raised a hand to tuck a stray lock of her long, pale blonde hair behind her ear gently, the soft touch of his warm fingers sending shivers tumbling down her spine. A pulse throbbed feverishly in her throat as his hand moved slowly down her neck, continuing on over her firm breast, whose tip hardened beneath his touch. Heat scorched through her trembling body, and she couldn't prevent herself from giving a quick gasp of pleasure at his intimate caress.

'Oh, yes...!' he breathed, his arms closing about her as, almost faint with dizziness, she swayed against the firm support of his hard figure. 'You want me, Angelica, every bit as much as I want you. It's useless to deny it,' he whispered, lowering his dark head until his lips were poised only a

fraction above her own, before softly and delicately tracing the outline of her mouth.

Angelica tried to steel herself, but she could feel
all her remaining resistance draining away beneath
the soft pressure of his lips. She was unable to tell
when the gentle, beguiling caress slowly changed to
a kiss of scorching, intense possession. Once again,
it seemed that from the moment his mouth touched
hers he was able effortlessly to tear down all her
carefully erected barriers, urgently compelling her
to surrender to the passionate response he was
demanding.

Reality seemed light-years away. She was only
conscious of the hard pressure of the thighs pressed
tightly to her own, her breasts crushed against his
muscular chest, and a driving force deep inside her,
clamouring for release, an overwhelming need to
respond to the powerfully seductive, deepening kiss
that feverishly tormented her senses.

Helplessly trapped like a moth by the flames of
her own need and desire, she could only respond
to the burning lips demanding her total sub-
mission. His kiss deepened until she was hardly able
to breathe, before he began slowly to release the
pressure.

As a shaft of late afternoon sunlight filtered
through the leaves of the tree, its deep glow dazzled
her eyes as they fluttered slowly open, her vision
filled by Luke's face only inches away from her
own. His hooded grey eyes were glittering with
aroused desire, a faint flush on the skin stretched
tightly over his high cheekbones and formidable
jawline; she saw the cruel sensuality of his lips as
he stared intently down at her for a moment.

'You don't need me to answer your question, do you?' he whispered huskily. 'Because we both know, only too well, what other reason I might have for wanting to marry you, hmm?'

Angelica's face burned, a deep tide of scarlet flooding over her pale cheeks at the recollection of just how she'd betrayed herself—yet again! As had happened so often in the past, she'd weakly allowed herself to fall under this man's spell—a man who was well aware of the power he had over her emotions.

But now it was a deadly, ultimately fatal power. Because, with all the shocking force of a thunderbolt, she suddenly realised that she'd been fooling herself for some time. She now *knew* that she was deeply and irrevocably in love with this man. A man who was only interested in her sexually, who she was very sure had no conception of the verb 'to love', and who appeared to believe that she was somehow up for sale to the highest bidder.

'L-lust may be a reason to get married, but it…it's not enough!' she cried, tearing herself from his arms and leaning helplessly against the wide trunk of the oak tree, desperately trying to come to terms with the shattering truth of her long-suppressed feelings.

He shrugged and gave a harsh, sardonic laugh. 'As far as I'm concerned, it will certainly do to be going on with!'

'But I could never…I couldn't possibly ever marry someone who wasn't truly and deeply in love with me!'

'Grow up, Angelica!' he rasped, gesturing with his hand towards the wall, the buzz of traffic along the Embankment clearly audible in the quiet garden. 'It's a hard, tough old world out there and lust—however much you may regret it—is a fact of life.'

'Yes, I know, but...'

'Lust exists. It's real. God knows, it's certainly tangible!' he continued relentlessly. 'But as for this "love" you speak about, you can't see, hear or touch it, can you? As far as I'm concerned, love is nothing but pure moonshine! It has about as much to do with real life as those fairy-stories my mother used to read to me when I was a small child.'

'Well, I don't care what you say!' she cried, wrapping her arms about her slim body, which was shivering uncontrollably with nervous tension. 'I'm not prepared to compromise. I'll never accept that lust or sexual attraction is enough to base a relationship on. Never!'

He stared at her, his granite-hard grey eyes beneath their heavy lids boring into hers, so that she felt as if her brain was being probed by an X-ray machine.

'Don't make the mistake of underestimating me, Angelica,' he said at last, his voice heavy with menace. 'Or of thinking that I am going just to walk away. Believe me—I don't give up that easily!'

'I don't want you—or your money!' she ground out through clenched teeth. 'So you can chat up Betty, or keep on knocking on my door, but I'm *not* going to change my mind.'

'Oh, yes, you will,' he told her with a supreme confidence which made her long to hit him. 'For instance, I don't think that you've thought matters through properly. What are you planning to do with Lady Marshall?'

'What do you mean? I don't intend to have anything more to do with the horrid old woman.'

He gave a bark of cruel laughter. 'I wouldn't count on it if I were you! In your shoes, I'd fully expect to be deluged by lawyer's letters any day now.'

'It won't work, Luke.' She lifted her chin scornfully towards him. 'So you can stop trying to frighten me, OK?'

'My dear girl, I wouldn't dream of doing anything of the sort,' he drawled smoothly, taking out his wallet and removing a visiting card, which he casually tucked into the pocket of her denim shirt. 'I'm quite prepared to wait for you to come to your senses. So when you change your mind—as I'm quite certain you will!—just give me a ring, hmm?'

'Go away!' she shouted furiously as he lowered his head to brush his mouth swiftly across her lips, before turning to walk away towards the garden gate.

'I . . . I wouldn't marry you—not if you were the last man on earth!' she yelled at his departing figure. 'I *won't* be bought or sold, like...like shares on the Stock Exchange. And if it means having to fight Lady Marshall on my own, that's just too bad! I don't need you, or your damn money!'

But the infuriating man merely gave a careless wave of his hand as he opened the garden gate, leaving only the sound of his sardonic laughter behind him as he disappeared from sight.

* * *

It seemed that Luke hadn't exaggerated the problems she would face, Angelica acknowledged with a heavy sigh, placing yet another large bill on the pile waiting for payment.

It was almost three weeks since he'd casually walked out of the garden, after his extraordinary proposal, and she was already almost at her wits' end, desperately wondering how to cope with her ever-increasing problems.

It wasn't just the lack of money which was so troubling, although it was a major contribution to her sleepless nights, when she would pace the floor desperately trying to decide which accounts to pay if and when she could find the money. A newly married, impecunious friend had once remarked that 'Happiness is not having to worry about the electricity and telephone bills'. And, although Angelica could remember laughing at the time, she was now able to appreciate fully just what her friend had meant.

However, as Luke had so accurately forecast, it was Lady Marshall who was proving to be her most troublesome adversary. There had been the expected letters from the trust's lawyers, of course. But, since the law seemed designed for delay, Angelica knew that she could stall matters for some considerable time. Unfortunately, there were many other sudden demands from officialdom which could not be so easily ignored.

Not that Lady Marshall had come out into the open, of course. But the awful old woman was clearly the primary malevolent influence behind the local council's sudden demand that, since Lonsdale House was open to the public, it must comply with goodness knew how many by-laws—most of which had been drawn up hundreds of years ago. And Angelica also suspected that the sudden arrival of a fire-inspection team could be laid at her door, as well as the detailed letters and stringent enquiries from both the local income tax and VAT offices.

All in all, the past weeks had been a nightmare.

The attitude of her old housekeeper and nanny hadn't helped either. Betty's temper seemed to be on a particularly short fuse these days, the ominous sound of crashing pots and pans down in the kitchen being the overture to muttered warnings about her leaving Lonsdale House. Angelica knew that the older woman wouldn't really put her dire threats into action, but now—when it was far too late—she dearly wished that she hadn't told Betty off about her underhand behaviour in sneakily letting Luke into the walled garden.

'There's none so blind as those in love,' Betty had snapped. 'Just because you're so damn stubborn and can't see beyond the end of your nose, there's no call to be so hoity-toity with me, my girl! If you want to look a gift horse in the mouth, and throw away a real chance of happiness, that's your look-out. Just don't come crying to me when he marries someone else, because I'll only say that it's all your own silly fault!'

Unfortunately, those few words had led to many more, ending in the worst quarrel they'd ever had, and leaving them both thoroughly upset.

And it had been no use her trying to escape by putting aside her problems for a few hours while acting as a guide for Footsteps in Time. Because— and this had probably been the most upsetting of all her recent trials and tribulations—David Webster had been unable to employ her any more.

'I'm sorry, Angelica,' he'd said with an unhappy shrug. 'But my new partner in the business absolutely insists that all our guides should hold a blue badge. So I'm afraid there's nothing I can do at the moment. However, I'm sure that it won't take you long to get one,' he'd added bracingly.

But they both knew that to gain a blue badge was very difficult indeed. It involved a tough, six-month training programme, followed by an even tougher exam held by the London Tourist Board. So it wasn't only a much coveted award, but also a solid guarantee to the public that they were in the safe hands of experts on the history and geography of London.

In fact it was her old schoolfriend, Kim, who'd been a tower of strength during these past weeks. But even she had been ruthlessly blunt when Angelica had visited her apartment at Chelsea Harbour for supper last night.

'I think you're mad!' Kim had said bluntly as she'd lifted the phone to order their meal to be delivered from a nearby Chinese restaurant. An arch-feminist to her fingertips, Kim resolutely refused to learn to cook, existing on frozen meals from the supermarket or take-away dishes from the many local restaurants—a fact which shocked Betty to the core.

'Why give yourself all this grief and hassle?' Kim had added, putting down the phone and pouring them both a glass of cold white wine. 'All you have to do is to phone Luke and tell him that you've changed your mind.'

'Are you insane, or what?' Angelica screeched, unable to believe that her fiercely independent friend could be giving her such feeble advice. 'Are you seriously suggesting that I should sell myself for filthy lucre? Because that's what it amounts to, you know. He appears to have only one thing on his mind, and it's a three letter word spelled S.E.X.!'

'So...?'

'What do you mean?'

Kim laughed. 'You don't fool me, kid. You're just crazy about him, right? And why not? He's spectacularly good-looking, as rich as Croesus, and a really amusing guy. What more do you want? Frankly, I'd advise you to grab him while the going's good.'

'I'm *not* crazy about him,' Angelica lied fiercely. 'Besides, when I marry, I want someone I can trust. And, believe me, Luke Cunningham is *supremely* untrustworthy.'

'Oh, come on—that just makes him more interesting,' Kim laughed. 'You've lived a damned boring life so far. I reckon you need a bit of excitement. And making sure that Mr Moneybags remains faithful and true would certainly keep you on your toes!'

'Kim! What on earth has come over you? How can you talk such nonsense!' Angelica wailed, gazing at her friend with disbelief. 'You've been such a good friend these past weeks. I was so sure...so certain that you'd somehow come up with an answer—or at least give me some good advice on how to cope with the situation.'

'Well, you're quite right, because I'm doing just that.' Kim put down her glass. 'Look here—you and I are as different as chalk from cheese, right? So what suits me would be no good for you, and vice versa. Now it seems that you've had the luck to find a man who wants to look after you—to take all the burdens off your shoulders, and smooth your path in life. I have to say,' she added with a laugh, 'that sort of set-up would drive me crazy. But you really love your dotty old house, and all those weird and wonderful curios in the museum. You want to continue living there until kingdom come—preferably with a loving husband, a horde of kids, and Betty whipping up calorie-laden culinary masterpieces in that awful old kitchen! Right?'

Angelica gave her a reluctant nod. 'Yes, I suppose you're right. But, even to achieve that sort of happiness, I couldn't possibly...I wouldn't dream of selling myself, in any way!'

'Of course you wouldn't,' Kim agreed. 'And nobody's asking you to. All you have to do is to stop being so damned stubborn and listen to your heart. I've known you most of my life, Angelica, and I'm as certain as I can be that you are madly in love with the guy. No—let me finish,' she said quickly as the other girl opened her mouth to protest.

'I know you say that he doesn't believe in love—but even the cleverest men can fool themselves about a thing like that. They can convince themselves that it's childish, and would somehow weaken them to admit the truth. But since you're mad about him, and he clearly fancies you rotten, he'll soon get around to seeing that love isn't such a bad thing after all!'

Sitting at her desk now, and staring down at the long white envelope which she'd just sealed ready for the post, Angelica realised just what a good friend she had in Kim.

Now that the other girl had made her face reality, Angelica knew that she'd wasted all this time denying her love for Luke—and to what purpose? She'd sent him away, and ever since his departure her life had been nothing but dust and ashes. Even if a fairy godmother had arrived, and waved a wand to solve all her problems, she'd still be feeling every bit as miserable and unhappy as she did at this minute.

But it had taken her a long time, trying to work out what she could possibly do about the situation. She really couldn't face having to call Luke on the telephone and tell him that she'd changed her mind. He might be in the middle of a business deal, for instance, and then she'd look all kinds of a fool. And, in any case, maybe she was too late? Maybe he'd got back together again with that awful Eleanor Nicholson?

At the thought of the beautiful dark accountant, Angelica had felt such a sharp pang of jealousy that she'd nearly doubled up in agony. She couldn't let that happen. She'd known that she must try and find a way to contact Luke, and yet not be seen as caving in too easily...

Continuing to stare down now at the thick envelope, she still found herself hesitating as to whether she should post it after all. Although she'd written the letter as carefully as possible, just simply acknowledging that she was willing to marry him, and not mentioning her feelings in any way, it was still a massive loss of face on her part. Could she cope with the humiliation if Luke chose to rub in that fact?

And then Angelica took a deep breath before quickly seizing up the letter. Jumping to her feet, she ran out of the study, across the hall and out of the door. Tearing down the street, her heart pounding with nerves, she knew that if she didn't put it in the postbox, which lay on the other side of the road, right this minute, she'd never again be able to find the courage to do so.

And that was why, without a sideways glance, she was racing blindly across the road—and why she neither saw nor heard the fast-approaching vehicle until it was far too late.

CHAPTER EIGHT

ANGELICA didn't like hospitals.

It wasn't really anything to do with the buildings themselves, she thought as she gazed around at the freshly painted cream décor. It was just that the stark walls, the bustling nurses and the sheer help-lessness of being trapped in an uncomfortable bed all reminded her so forcefully of her only previous visit to such an institution.

When, aged ten, she had suddenly developed acute appendicitis, only a few weeks after her mother and father's death in a car crash, she'd been whisked by ambulance into the nearest hospital. There, amid all the pain of the operation itself, together with her naked misery and anguish at the loss of her beloved parents, she had spent some of the most miserable days of her young life. Even now, it only needed the pungent smell of antiseptic to take her straight back to that grief-stricken, des-perately unhappy time.

Muttering grumpily under her breath, she tried to make herself more comfortable. But with her left leg in plaster, from her ankle to halfway up her thigh, it was proving to be a difficult task.

Although there was no doubt that she'd been very lucky, Angelica was heartily sick of everyone telling her that she'd had a miraculous escape from certain death. Mainly, she supposed, because she was so

ashamed of having behaved like a small child, in
dashing across the road without having the sense
to keep an eye out for traffic. Foolishly careless,
she'd neither seen nor heard the car with which
she'd collided, nor had she any real recollection of
what had happened after that, until groggily waking
up in this hospital bed with a splitting headache
and her leg in plaster.

However, it was due to the fact that she'd been
unconscious for some time that the doctors had
insisted on her remaining here, so that they could
carry out a number of tests. And, until they were
quite convinced that she was well enough to go
home, here she had to stay.

'I'm perfectly well,' she'd told the young house-
man earlier in the day. 'I've only got a broken leg,
for heaven's sake!'

'Don't worry. We'll get you out of here just as
soon as we can. Believe me, we need the bed!' he'd
grinned, before adding his name and a small
drawing to the others on her plaster cast. 'If all
goes well, you can probably leave tomorrow
morning,' he'd added, before dashing off to see to
another patient.

Glancing down at her watch, Angelica gave a
heavy sigh and lay back on the pillows. It was
almost visiting time, and Betty should be here any
minute. At least then she might learn what had been
going on at Lonsdale House in her absence. The
garbled phone call yesterday had been thoroughly
unsatisfactory. Her old housekeeper had appeared
to be strangely excited, and full of heavy hints about
a change in all their fortunes. But other than won-

dering whether Betty had at last managed to back a winner—an unlikely event, since the elderly housekeeper always seemed to put her money on horses with only three good legs and a tendency to come in last—Angelica didn't have a clue what was going on.

However, she'd had plenty of visitors, including both Kim and David Webster, but, although they had been kind enough to bring her fruit and bunches of flowers, nothing could match the enormous bouquet of crimson roses which had arrived yesterday afternoon.

Glancing at the huge vase on her bedside table, filled with blooms whose heady scent seemed able to banish even the smell of antiseptic, she reached over to pick up the card which had accompanied the roses. It was an exact replica of the small, by now rather creased and crumpled white business card which Luke had tucked into her pocket over three weeks ago. There was no signature and no message. Only the delivery of the bouquet acknowledged the fact that he'd obviously heard about her accident, and that he must know she was now in hospital.

What else did you expect? she asked herself roughly. It had, after all, been kind of Luke to send her these magnificent flowers. So it was stupid to keep on wishing that he'd taken the trouble either to write a short note, or personally sign his business card. And it was probably just as well that he hadn't paid her a visit. What would she have said to him if he had? Besides, although the bruise on the side of her face was slowly beginning to fade at last, she would hate to have him see her look so awful!

In fact, since she obviously hadn't managed to post her letter—and he'd therefore had no reason to try and contact her—Angelica was still wondering how Luke had heard the news that she was in hospital. And what *had* happened to her letter? It would be hideously embarrassing if it had been picked up and read by anyone else. She'd tried questioning various people, including Betty, but no one seemed to have any recollection of a long white envelope lying on the road at the scene of the accident. So, like many other things in life, she told herself gloomily, it had undoubtedly been swept up by the rubbish collectors, and——

'Well! You look like a wet weekend and no mistake!' Betty's voice broke through her dismal thoughts, and she turned to see her old nanny standing beside the bed, beaming down at her with a broad smile.

'Never mind, you look cheerful enough for both of us,' Angelica muttered glumly, sighing as she levered herself up against the pillows. 'What's happened? Don't tell me that you've actually managed to back a winner for the first time in your life?'

'Ooo, no, something *much* better than that!' she told the girl excitedly, swaying slightly as she turned to look for a chair, before dragging it up to the bed.

'Have you been drinking?' Angelica demanded incredulously, gazing at Betty's flushed red face in astonishment as her nostrils became aware of the sharp, pungent smell of whisky fumes.

'Well, what if I have?' Her old nanny laughed. 'You just wait until you hear what I've got to tell you—and then see if you don't feel like breaking out the champagne as well!'

However, by the time Betty had finished relating her startling piece of news, Angelica wasn't at all sure *how* she felt. Her brooding silence went unremarked upon by the older woman, who was too carried away by euphoria—and whisky—to notice anything amiss.

'You could have knocked me down with a feather,' Betty said for the umpteenth time, taking a small flask from her bag and tipping another slug of alcohol down her throat. 'I've never been so gobsmacked in all my life! If only I could see the expression on Lady Marshall's face when she hears the news—talk about a laugh! Serve the old cow right, that's what I say,' she added with a loud hiccup.

'Look here, I think you've probably had enough of that stuff,' Angelica told her sternly, leaning over to take the flask from Betty's hands, and putting it firmly back into the older woman's handbag. 'And for goodness' sake take a taxi home. You'll never manage to get yourself on a bus—not in your present state.'

'You could be right,' Betty giggled, before giving the girl a kiss, and making her way unsteadily out of the ward.

Someone had once told Angelica that there were far more extraordinary coincidences to be found in real life than in fiction. After what Betty had just been telling her, she could well believe it! For it now appeared that the missing heiress, who shared the inheritance of Lonsdale House with Angelica, had been traced at long last.

But it seemed a particularly cruel twist of fate to discover that Mrs Elizabeth Eastman had apparently died well over a year ago. So Angelica would never know if the American woman—whom she'd never met—might have enjoyed either Sir Tristram's old house or its unusual contents. However, she *did* know that the dead woman's only child, a son by her first marriage, was very much alive. Astonishing as it might seem, it was *Luke Cunningham* who had now inherited a half-share in Lonsdale House!

'It appears that he knew nothing about a possible inheritance,' Betty had explained. 'Not until he was sitting in our kitchen some weeks ago, and you was telling him all about the missing American lady, Mrs Eastman, and how you was trying to track her down. And it's no wonder the poor woman couldn't be found, seeing as how she was dead all the time. It seems a crying shame, doesn't it?' Betty had sighed, taking another sip from her flask.

'Anyway, as I was saying, Mr Cunningham told me that the reason he didn't say anything at the time was because he reckoned there must be thousands of people by that name in the United States. But he got his lawyers on to it, and now it seems he owns the other half of the house. How about *that*?' Betty had laughed happily.

How about that, indeed! Angelica thought, lying in her hospital bed later that night, and staring blindly up through the darkness at the ceiling.

Of course, it had to be good news as far as Lonsdale House itself was concerned. There would be nothing to stop Luke spending his money on bringing the old place into the twentieth century, employing a curator, and generally putting the museum in good order. And, of course, never again would Lady Marshall be able to dictate terms or crack the financial whip quite so stringently as she'd done in the past.

But there was another side of the coin, about which she was not so happy—a large question mark hanging over *her* future. Because there was now nothing to stop Luke from doing very much as he pleased with Lonsdale House. And the thought suddenly occurred to Angelica that she might well have exchanged one dominant personality for another. Only Luke was likely to be a whole lot tougher and far more difficult to cope with than horrid old Lady Marshall.

However, it was the situation regarding her relationship with Luke which was first and foremost in her mind.

On the one hand, it was a relief to know that there was no mystery about how he'd discovered that she was in hospital. Since he'd obviously been in touch with Betty over the past two days, the older woman was bound to have told him all about the accident. But... she and Luke had parted on such bad terms that even now—all these weeks later— she could feel her cheeks reddening at the recollection of her furiously angry words. It was, to say the least, going to be both extremely awkward and embarrassing having to face him once again.

In the event, and to her great relief, it proved to be not nearly as awkward as she had feared.

It had been very kind of Luke to send his chauffeur, Colin, to pick her up from the hospital, Angelica mused the next morning. Luckily, Betty had provided her with a crisp cotton dress and a matching cardigan in her favourite colour of sapphire-blue. And she'd also managed to wash her long hair before leaving the hospital. All of which helped her to feel slightly more confident when she arrived home to find Luke waiting to help her up the steps of Lonsdale House.

As he greeted her with a friendly smile and came to her aid, giving her some good advice as she struggled with the unfamiliar crutches, Angelica found their meeting much easier than she'd imagined. She was, in fact, very grateful for his steady arm, which prevented her from falling on the slippery floor of the hall, and the care with which he guided her into the study.

'You must be exhausted. Would you like a drink?' he asked as she tried to settle herself comfortably into a high-backed chair beside the fireplace.

'No—um—just coffee, please,' she muttered breathlessly, bending down to place her crutches on the floor, deliberately allowing the silken weight of her long blonde hair to shield her flushed face from his view.

'Is you leg very sore?' he asked, coming back into the room with two mugs of coffee.

'No. It was at first, of course, but now I can't really feel very much. It's just this cast which sometimes drives me up the wall,' she explained. 'I nearly go mad when my leg begins to itch, because there's no way of doing anything about it—not with this heavy lump of plaster in the way!'

'I've got the solution to that little problem,' he said, and when she looked at him in surprise he explained that he knew exactly what she was going through. 'When my shinbone was smashed in a college game of football—I'm talking about American football, which is more like English rugger—my mother came up with the idea of using one of her knitting needles so that I could scratch my leg. It really worked, and kept me sane!' He grinned. 'We'll have to see if Betty has any knitting tucked away somewhere.'

Angelica hesitated for a minute, not quite knowing what to say, but realising that in mentioning his mother he'd given her the opportunity to raise the subject.

'I was so sorry to hear about your mother. I had no idea that it was only recently that she'd died. Were you—er—were you very close?'

'When I was much younger and living in the States, we certainly saw a lot of one another. Like any mother and son, I suppose. Although I very much regret that we hadn't seen a lot of each other over the past few years. I was generally too tied up in business over here to be able to spend much time at home in America.' He shrugged.

'Do you have any brothers or sisters?'

He shook his dark head. 'No. I was her only child. She and my stepfather—of whom, incidentally, I was very fond—never had any children of their own. It was quite a shock, standing at her graveside and realising that I no longer had any living relatives—that I was finally alone in the world,' he mused quietly. 'Maybe that's what started me thinking about my present way of life?'

Remembering their last, very acrimonious conversation in the garden, which had been mainly concerned with his desire to re-think his lifestyle, Angelica quickly diverted their conversation towards the matter of his new inheritance.

'Betty and I were both amazed to hear that you're the missing heir to this house. We're absolutely— er—delighted by the news, of course,' she added hurriedly, slightly thrown when she saw his shoulders shaking with laughter.

'According to Betty, I understand that the correct word is gobsmacked!' he grinned. 'I'm afraid that the poor old girl has been suffering from a dreadful migraine this morning. Which is why I saw to our coffee.'

'I think you'll find that Betty is suffering from nothing more than a raging hangover,' Angelica told him drily. 'After celebrating your good news, she was practically as drunk as a skunk when she came to see me in hospital yesterday. Quite frankly, I'm amazed that she managed to find her way home!'

He laughed, and then lapsed into silence for a moment, seemingly buried deep in thought.

For her part, Angelica fiddled nervously with her empty coffee-mug, wondering what on earth to say or do next. Although she'd never really had any serious doubts in the matter, it was now fairly obvious that Luke *hadn't* received her letter. And therefore he could have no idea that she'd caved in over the question of their marriage. So, where did they go from here?

Luke had been very pleasant and friendly so far. And if she hadn't been able to recall vividly their last explosive meeting, there wouldn't be any problem. Unfortunately, with his tall figure lounging in a chair across the room, she couldn't seem to rid her mind of everything they'd said to each other on that occasion—or the memory of that passionate kiss. Just the sight of the slim-fitting dark trousers over those long legs, and the broad shoulders covered by a soft grey cashmere sweater over a casual, open-necked shirt, was enough to set her heart pounding like a tom-tom.

The sound of Luke clearing his throat brought her sharply back down to earth.

'I realise that I should have said something to you when you first mentioned my mother's name, a few weeks ago,' he said with an apologetic smile. 'However, it quickly occurred to me that, since Eastman is not an uncommon name, I ought to make sure of my facts before taking any action.'

'Yes, I...I quite understand,' she muttered breathlessly, trying to pull herself together.

'However, now that I hear we are joint owners of this crazy house, there will be much to talk about. And I think I ought to tell you straight away that you have nothing more to fear from Lady Marshall.'

'I'm delighted to hear it!'

'I had a long—er—in-depth conversation with the old lady yesterday,' Luke said blandly. 'And

I'm sure you will be pleased to know that she has—after, I must admit, a certain amount of arm-twisting!—resigned from the board of trustees, and appointed myself in her place.'

Angelica gave him a nervous smile. 'I'm obviously thankful that you've got rid of the awful old woman. But I'm still a bit confused . . . I mean, what happens now?'

'I can't see any point in rushing into any decisions,' he told her firmly. 'I suggest that we just take things easy, and work it out as we go along. In the first instance, and because of your accident, I've taken two weeks' leave from my office. I've had to install a fax machine, of course——' he nodded to a large square object on the desk by the window '—but otherwise I'm quite confident that my staff can carry on as usual during my stay here.'

'Your stay here . . . ?' she echoed, gazing at him in bewilderment. 'You don't mean . . . surely you can't be expecting to—er—live here, in this house?'

'My dear girl, of course I am,' he drawled, raising a quizzical dark eyebrow, as though surprised that she should even query the fact. 'There are, after all, at least six spare bedrooms, are there not?'

'Yes, well—um—we do have plenty of room,' she reluctantly agreed, disturbed by her immediate, instinctive reaction of dismay.

It might be totally irrational, but she deeply resented the fact that this man was already making himself at home in Lonsdale House. It was . . . well, it was a sort of invasion of her territory. She was just trying to think of several good reasons for him to remain in his own apartment when his next words shot all of her half-formed arguments down in flames.

'With your leg in plaster, you can hardly show visitors around the house,' he pointed out with devastating logic. 'And I really feel that it's asking too much of poor Betty—who'll have her hands full looking after you—to have to deal with members of the public, on top of everything else.'

'It won't be long before I'm able to get around. I feel perfectly well,' she retorted.

'I'm sure you do. But, since you must be tired on your first day out of hospital, I'm now going to carry you upstairs to bed,' he said firmly as he rose to his feet.

She gritted her teeth. 'There's absolutely no need for you to do anything of the sort. With these crutches, I'm perfectly well able to look after myself!'

But he took not a blind bit of notice of her protests as he quickly scooped her up in his arms. Even the heavy plaster cast didn't seem to make any difference to the consummate ease with which he was able to handle her angry, protesting figure.

'You'd better keep still,' he warned as he paused at the foot of the stairs. 'If you fall and smash that cast, it will only mean having another one fitted. So why don't you hold on—and shut up?'

The threat of having to return to hospital was enough to make Angelica realise that it was useless to argue any further.

Nervously she put her hands about his neck, a flush spreading over her pale skin at the warmth of the hard, firm arms clasped about her trembling body. With her face so close to his, her nostrils seemed filled with his own musky, masculine scent, mingled with the aromatic perfume of his cologne. Quickly clamping her eyes tightly shut, before she gave in to a sudden, mad desire to run her fingers through his thick, dark hair, or to press her lips to the sculptured hollow beneath his prominent cheekbone, Angelica desperately struggled to control her body, which seemed to be shaking like a leaf.

'There you are, you should be more comfortable here,' he said, entering her bedroom and lowering her gently down on the wide bed. 'I'll send Betty up to help you undress.'

'I'm not tired, I don't need to be undressed, and I *really* don't want to be stuck up here for the rest of the day, either! Where are my crutches?'

'They're downstairs, of course.'

'Well, I'm obviously going to need them, aren't I?' she pointed out, practically grinding her teeth as he slowly shook his head.

'Later, maybe. When you've had a good sleep.'

So, OK, she was feeling far more tired than she was prepared to admit. But he had no right to dump her up here, like an unwanted parcel. And without her crutches she was completely stuck!

'Now, why don't you just try to relax?' he told her in a calm, irritatingly patient voice. 'I understand that you had a very nasty bump on your head. So, we don't want you doing too much, too soon— do we?'

'I may have a broken leg but the doctors say that my *head* is in perfect working order!' she snapped.

How dared he talk to her as if she were a dim-witted, fractious child?

Furious with herself at being so easily out-manoeuvred, she glared up at Luke, who was continuing to regard her with an impassively calm, bland expression on his face. But she wasn't fooled—not for one minute! She was perfectly well aware, from the deep gleam of sardonic mockery in his glittering grey eyes, that he was deriving considerable amusement from her obvious annoyance and frustration.

How *could* she have ever imagined that she was in love with this truly *awful* man?

'How much longer have I got to put up with this rotten plaster cast?' Angelica muttered, giving a heavy sigh as she put down her book.

'I'm sure it won't be long before it's off,' Betty murmured soothingly as she finished dusting the desk in the study. 'And Mr Cunningham has promised to try and get you a lighter cast just as soon as he comes back from New York,' she added. 'So cheer up! It's probably just all this rain what's making you feel so blue.'

She might be right, Angelica thought, turning to look at the raindrops cascading down the window-pane. Although nothing seemed to dampen Betty's spirits these days. Happy as a sandboy to have Luke around the house—especially as he enthusiastically wolfed down every delicious meal she set before him—the older woman was irritatingly bright and cheerful, singing old music hall songs as she went

about her work, and generally driving Angelica
around the bend.

It seemed strange not to have Luke around. But
his few days away in America on business might
give her an opportunity to get her head together.
For the first time, it occurred to her that it might
be the stress and strain of having to live cheek by
jowl with Luke which had been making her feel so
depressed lately. And she didn't even have the satisfaction of being able to complain about the way
he was treating her. How could she, when he was
always polite and considerate, and generally be-
having like a distant if pleasant stranger?

Goodness knew, she ought to be glad that his
attitude towards her was like . . . well, like the way
he might treat a sister. But trying to keep her own
deep feelings for him under some sort of control
was becoming more and more difficult with every
passing day. And, unfortunately, the situation
wasn't helped by the fact that he'd never, ever referred to his original proposal of marriage.

But why should he, she reminded herself glumly,
when he now had a perfect right to live in this
house? After all, he'd only suggested that they
marry in order to solve her difficulties with the
house and Lady Marshall. So there was no need to
go to those lengths now. Not when, to all intents
and purposes, the problems had already been removed from her shoulders.

Angelica didn't much like herself these days.
Surely she never used to be so discontented and
wretchedly unhappy, or feeling incredibly restless

and depressed—as if she were somehow an alien in what had once been her own private home.

There was no doubt that things had certainly changed! Luke had already interviewed several applicants for the post of curator. He'd also been arranging for builders to submit estimates for the repair of the roof, and for redecorating the whole house from top to bottom. Betty was to have a new kitchen, and there were plans to double the number of bathrooms.

It was obvious that Luke was extremely efficient, and she couldn't quarrel with any of his plans for modernising the house. But, other than being asked to rubber-stamp his decisions, Angelica felt that she'd hardly been consulted on all these changes. And, since Luke now had a legal share in her inheritance, she could hardly object to his plans.

Strangely enough, one of the few bright aspects of her present-day existence was her new friendship with Norma, Luke's secretary and personal assistant.

Often calling at the house with important business, the middle-aged woman and Angelica would often sit chatting together over a cup of coffee, while waiting for Luke to read and sign documents. And Angelica had been touched when, after complaining that she hadn't anything to read, Norma had returned the next day with a bag full of torrid romances.

'For goodness' sake, don't tell Mr Cunningham,' Norma had muttered as she'd handed them to the girl. 'Most men think these sort of books are silly.

But, as you're stuck with nothing to do, they may help to pass the time.'

'I'm very grateful—and I promise not to lend them to Luke!' Angelica had giggled, staring fascinated at some of the amazingly lurid illustrations on the covers of the books.

They had indeed helped to pass the time while she waited for her leg to heal. Unfortunately, reading about hot, sensual passion and unbridled lust only made matters worse somehow, increasing the acute frustration and unhappiness she felt over her hopeless love for Luke.

Her dismal reverie was interrupted by the sound of the doorbell.

Realising that Betty had intended to go out shopping after doing the housework, she got up out of her chair. She'd become used to her crutches by now, and had no trouble making her way across the hall. Pulling the front door open, she was stunned to discover Eleanor Nicholson standing on the doorstep.

'May I come in?' Eleanor murmured, not giving Angelica a chance to say no, as she slipped past the girl balancing awkwardly on her crutches and made her way into the hall.

'What a charming house!'

'Thank you,' Angelica replied stonily. 'What can I do for you?'

'Eleanor gave a tinkling laugh. 'I think you've got that the wrong way around. It's what I can do for *you* which has brought me here today.'

'Oh, really?' Angelica murmured, realising that her instinctive dislike of the dark-haired woman the one and only time they'd met each other, at the Ritz hotel, was still as strong as ever.

'Why don't we sit down and have a little talk?' Eleanor suggested sweetly. 'Luke tells me that you're really doing *splendidly* on those crutches of yours. But it must be tiring to be on your feet for too long.'

'No—I think I'd like you to go, and...'

But Angelica found that she was speaking to herself, as Eleanor had already left the dark hall, and was now making herself at home in the study.

'Damn cheek!' she muttered grimly under her breath. But, since there was no point in standing out here on her own, she was reluctantly forced to join the dark-haired girl in the other room.

'Luke's told me such a lot about this house!' Eleanor exclaimed as she looked about her. 'As I told him when we went to the opera last week, he really must...' She paused, staring at the girl who'd just given a strangled gasp. 'Didn't you know about our date last week? Oh, dear—I can see that Luke didn't tell you. Wasn't that naughty of him?'

'It wasn't a date,' Angelica protested. 'It was corporate entertainment. And Luke didn't take me, because he hates opera. He said that he always falls asleep, and he reckoned I would too.'

'Oh, is *that* what he told you?' Eleanor laughed. 'I don't suppose he mentioned that he took me out to dinner afterwards? Well, never mind. You can ask him all about it when he gets back from New York, can't you?'

Angelica tried to cling on to her knowledge of Luke. She might have fought and raged at him, but she knew that he would never lie to her. But, on the other hand, he *had* been to the opera, and he *had* returned very late. And, most worrying of all, how did Eleanor know that he was in New York, if he hadn't told her himself?

'Of course, I did wonder if he hadn't bitten off more than he could chew with this house,' the other girl was saying as she walked around the room. 'But, now he's taken over the chairmanship of the trust, it all makes perfect sense. Poor old Aunt Doreen—what a tiresome woman!' she added with a laugh. 'But I *am* her only relative, and with all that wealth ... So useful, if you see what I mean?'

'You mean that you're nice to the beastly old dragon just because you want to inherit her money,' Angelica replied scornfully.

'Precisely!' Eleanor gave another of her irritating, tinkling laughs. 'Anyway, it all seems to have worked out splendidly, doesn't it? Luke's in here now—and you, alas, are well and truly out.'

'Oh, no, I'm not!' Angelica ground out forcefully. 'I have a legal half-share in this house. I'm entitled to live here as long as I like.'

'Ah, I don't think that's *quite* right,' Eleanor murmured, gazing at her reflection in the large gilt mirror over the fireplace. 'I think, if I recall the trust deed correctly—and, of course, I do!—that you are only allowed to live in this house with the permission of the trustees.'

'So what?' Angelica snapped.

Eleanor shook her lovely head in mock-sorrow. 'Don't be so dim, sweetie! Surely you must remember the very first action of Luke's, when he knew he'd inherited this amazing place?'

'He only inherited a *half*-share in "this amazing place",' Angelica corrected her grimly through gritted teeth.

'He went to see Aunt Doreen, didn't he?' Eleanor continued blithely, ignoring the blonde girl's interruption. 'And when he left *he* was the new chairman of the trustees, right?'

'Yes, but...but...' Angelica's voice died slowly away.

'Ah—I see the penny has dropped at last!' Eleanor laughed. 'Isn't my darling Luke a clever, clever man? Never misses a trick, does he? Of course, he's really been very kind, letting you stay on here after coming out of hospital. Poor old you,' she added, looking down at the cast. 'It must be terribly uncomfortable.'

'You can cut out the false sympathy,' Angelica told her grimly. 'And if you or Luke think that I'm going to leave this house—the only home I've ever known—you're very much mistaken!'

Eleanor smiled. 'You really are living in a fool's paradise, aren't you? Do you really imagine that the other trustees will oppose their very rich, very influential new chairman? And if he says that he and I are getting married, that we want the house to ourselves...? Well, I don't think the trustees will give him too much hassle, do you?'

'I...I don't believe he'd ever do that—throw me out of the house, I mean. And I don't...don't believe he's going to marry you, either!' Angelica cried, still desperately trying to cling on to her sanity. All these things that Eleanor was saying—they couldn't possibly be true, could they?

Eleanor shrugged. 'Men are such ruthless bastards, aren't they? I told Luke not to be so hard on you—to give you time to leave of your own accord, instead of being thrown out by the trustees. But I'm afraid that I didn't have much luck. When we were discussing this matter in bed, just the other night, Luke said that——'

'You were *what* . . . ?' Angelica gasped, unable to believe what she was hearing. 'I . . . I don't believe it!'

'What don't you believe?' Eleanor queried sweetly. 'That we were discussing business, or that we were in bed together? My dear girl, Luke and I are great believers in combining business and pleasure!' She laughed. 'There's no need to look so shocked. Didn't you know that Luke and I have been lovers for simply *years*? I must admit that we've both been such workaholics that it didn't seem important to get married. But now Luke has decided to settle down and bring up his family in this house . . . well, it all makes sense, doesn't it?'

'Get out of here!' Angelica cried, clasping her hands to her ears, and trying not to listen any more to this evil, amoral woman.

'No, sweetie. It's *you* who are going to have to get out of here.' Eleanor shook her head sorrowfully. 'I'm sorry, but Luke asked me to bring the bad news to you while he's away in New York. I'm flying out to join him tonight, actually. He says that he's going mad—he just can't *wait* to make love to me. Isn't that sweet of him?'

Angelica couldn't prevent herself from giving a deep, heart-wrenching wail of despair as she suddenly doubled up with pain and anguish.

'Now, now, there's no need to cry, sweetie. We all have to grow up one day, you know, and it's about time that you joined the real world! So I'll tell darling Luke that I kept my promise to see you. But if you're still here when he comes back, well——' she shrugged '—he's just going to have to do his own dirty work, isn't he? And now,' she added, glancing down at her watch, 'I really must dash to catch the plane.'

Eleanor was just turning to the door when she stopped and gave another of her peals of laughter.

'Oh, silly me—how *could* I have forgotten?' she said, turning around and taking a long white creased and crumpled envelope from her handbag. 'I really think you ought to have this back. Although I must say Luke and I were screaming with laughter when he read it out loud to me a few weeks ago. I mean, it isn't usually a woman who writes proposing marriage to a man, is it? Luke said it gave him the best laugh he'd had for years!'

Angelica, her skin crawling with humiliation, could only stare with horror-struck, dazed eyes at the other woman as she tossed the letter down on to a table, before throwing the trembling girl a brilliant, glittering smile and sweeping out of the door into the hall.

Frozen, unable to move her body and shivering with tension, Angelica heard the front door slam. As the loud sound reverberated in her ears like a mourning bell, she stared at the long white envelope, desperately trying to come to terms with the fact that the whole of her world had just been smashed to pieces—totally devastated and destroyed beyond repair.

CHAPTER NINE

'Now, for goodness' sake, Angelica, please *don't* try practising your non-existent cooking skills.' Kim laughed as she sped around the flat, picking up her briefcase, jacket and handbag. 'I'll bring us home something to eat tonight, OK?'

'It was just that I haven't got anything to do all day,' Angelica murmured.

'Yes, I know. But the kitchen still smells of burnt pastry after your last attempt at apple pie. So try and control yourself—right?' Kim grinned. 'I'll get some Chinese take-away, and then we can poison ourselves on monosodium glutamate instead! See you later, kid. And *do* try not to mope too much.'

Angelica waited until Kim had left her apartment before limping disconsolately back into the spare bedroom to try and find some aspirins.

A victim of painful, tense headaches, she could do nothing, it seemed, to banish Luke from her mind—no matter how desperately hard she tried to do so. He was her first thought on waking and her last at night, his tall, dark presence invading even her disturbed, restless sleep and torturous nightmares.

Never in all her life had she known such misery. It was almost impossible to describe the agony of mind and body which seemed to have her in thrall. Ever since that horrendous visit from what must

169

be one of the most evil women she'd ever met, her whole life had become a desperately lonely, wretched state of purgatory—an arid, lonely desert where nothing seemed capable of lifting the heavy weight of her deep unhappiness and despair.

Maybe she wouldn't entirely have believed Eleanor, if it hadn't been for that letter. But it was the sight of the stained and crumpled white envelope which had hammered the final nail into her coffin. Clearly someone must have picked it up in the road and put it into the postbox, since on examining the envelope it was obvious that the letter had been through the postal system. Which meant that it *had* been delivered to Luke's apartment, and he must have known about what she'd written all the time he'd been staying at Lonsdale House.

There seemed absolutely no sane, sensible reason why he'd never mentioned receiving the letter. Nor why he'd treated her in such a distant, almost uncaring manner after her return from hospital. In fact, the *only* reason that made any kind of sense at all was that Eleanor really had been speaking the truth. That Luke had been toying with her emotions all along, and that he'd only originally proposed marriage to get his hands on Lonsdale House.

Angelica couldn't, of course, believe that he was seriously at all interested in Sir Tristram's collection—especially since he'd never had anything but a faintly amused, mocking attitude towards the exhibits. But there was no doubt that the house was situated in a very desirable locality and, together with its large garden, would fetch well over a million pounds on the open market. So...maybe that was

Luke and Eleanor's next move? Having gained control of the trust, maybe they were planning to destroy the collection and sell Lonsdale House—the only home she'd ever known—for as much money as they could get...?

But such unhappy thoughts were as nothing compared with Luke's apparent cruel abandonment of her—or the fact that he'd merely set out to capture her heart for sordid, mercenary reasons, and to provide some amusement for both himself and his girlfriend.

The ghastly humiliation and shame were still as sharp and painful as they had been four days ago. Shivering with shock and distress, she had taken an age to pull herself together. And, even then, she'd been able to do nothing more than grab her handbag and stagger out of the house on her crutches, before hailing a taxi and asking to be driven to Kim's apartment in Chelsea Harbour.

What she would have done without the help and support of her friend she had absolutely no idea. Although Kim firmly believed that Eleanor must be lying, even she had had to admit—after Angelica had produced the letter—that the evidence against Luke was almost overwhelming. However, she'd faithfully promised not to contact either him or Betty.

Unfortunately, with nothing to do and nowhere to go, Angelica had been drifting through the past four days in a total state of shock. Time seemed to drag interminably, and, although she did her best to spin out the tedious hours of her day, there were long periods of time when she had nothing to do but think about her love for Luke, a man who'd been clearly exposed as a cheat and a liar.

Taking as long as possible to have a leisurely bath—she had, by now, become adept at managing to cope with her heavy plaster cast—and wash her long, pale blonde hair, she was surprised to see that it was still only eleven o'clock, with the day stretching interminably out before her. However, just as she was deciding that she must get dressed, Angelica heard a buzz from the security phone operated by the guard downstairs from his desk in the front hall of the apartment block.

'It's Davidson here, miss. I've got a large parcel for Miss Kim Edwards, and, since it says "perishable food" on the carton, I reckon I'd better bring it up straight away.'

'Yes, all right,' she murmured dully.

Kim had impressed on her the importance of never letting anyone in without checking first with the security guard—and even then being very careful. However, she knew Davidson's voice, and, beyond vaguely wondering what sort of food Kim had bought, she had no qualms as she responded to the ring of the doorbell.

Using a heavy walking stick provided by Kim, she limped slowly down the hall, trying to be careful not to trip on the hem of the long white silk dressing-gown which she'd borrowed from her friend. And, even then, it took Angelica some time to undo the various locks fixed to the front door, which always made her feel as if she was living inside Fort Knox.

Although, after opening the door, she immediately tried to slam it shut again, her puny strength and awkwardness with her plaster cast were no match for the superior force of the hard, tall figure on the other side of the door.

'Thank you, Davidson.' Luke Cunningham grinned, keeping his foot jammed in the door as he tucked a fifty-pound note into the breast pocket of the guard's uniform, before taking the large parcel from him. 'You've performed a signal service today.'

'No, he hasn't!' Angelica cried. 'He's just sold himself for filthy lucre!'

'Yes, miss, I'm afraid you're quite right!' Davidson grinned, before assuring Luke that he would keep an eye on both the limousine and its chauffeur, parked outside the apartment block. 'And good luck, sir,' he told Luke. 'I remember when I was courting. I used to have the same trouble with the old woman. Don't you stand any nonsense—that's my advice to you.'

'I'll try and remember that,' Luke replied with grim amusement, before kicking the door shut with his foot, and carrying the parcel past Angelica's trembling figure and through into the main sitting-room of the apartment.

'Come on—where's the kitchen?' he demanded, putting the parcel down on a table and pulling out two bottles of champagne, a side of smoked salmon and several small pots of caviare. 'Hurry up,' he added impatiently. 'These bottles of champagne have already been chilled—and my hands are freezing!'

Angelica was so shocked and stunned that she found herself weakly showing Luke into the small kitchen.

'That's better,' he muttered a few minutes later as he removed the cork from a champagne bottle with a satisfactory 'plop'. 'Drink up!' he said, holding out a glass towards her.

'No!' she cried, finally breaking out of her shocked, trance-like state. 'No... Get out of here!' she added, frantically tightening the belt of the thin silk robe about her naked body.

'Drink up—or I'll ram it down your stupid throat!' he growled, firmly placing the glass in her trembling hand.

'How... how dare you? Don't you *ever* talk to me like that!'

'I'm a *very* angry man at the moment—so don't mess with me!' he retorted savagely. 'Besides, I reckon I can talk to my future wife in any way I like!'

'What... what did you say?' she gasped, almost unable to believe her ears.

'Don't you realise that I've been driven nearly demented ever since I returned from New York two days ago?' he demanded angrily, draining his glass and taking no notice of her breathless query. 'No one knew what had happened to you, or where you'd got to. I've been in contact with the police, most of the hospitals in London and even, God help me, the Salvation Army!' he exploded, spinning on his heel and hurling his empty glass into the fire-place, where it lay shattered in tiny pieces.

There was a long, shocked silence for a moment, before Angelica gave a helpless shake of her head. 'I...I didn't mean...I didn't know...'

'What *on earth* possessed you to be so silly?' he roared, gripping hold of her shoulders and giving her such a fierce shake that her champagne was flung out of the glass and down on to the carpet. 'I've been nearly driven out of my mind with worry and despair!'

'Eleanor came... She said...'

He swore grimly under his breath. 'I still can't understand how you could have believed her evil lies. For God's sake, Angelica—don't you know and trust me *at all*?'

'How...how do you know what Eleanor said to me?' she cried.

'Because Kim has given me a blow-by-blow account of exactly what went on—that's how,' he told her harshly. 'And, before you start taking your anger out on your oldest friend, I can tell you that she did *not* get in touch with me. I rang her—as I've rung every single one of your friends and acquaintances—every damn name in the address book you left behind, in fact. OK?'

'No, of course it's not OK,' she shouted, the shock beginning to wear off, and raging anger quickly taking its place. 'How do I know that you aren't planning to get rid of me, just as Eleanor said? Ever since I came back from hospital, you've treated me as though I...I had some kind of nasty, infectious disease!'

Luke groaned. 'May the good Lord give me strength! Have you forgotten that you'd nearly been killed in that accident?' he ground out fiercely. 'Not to mention that you'd also had a nasty blow to the head, *and* that your leg was in plaster! What on earth was I supposed to do? Leap on a sick girl, and enjoy having my wicked way with someone who'd just come out of hospital?'

'Well... well, no—I suppose not, but...'

'I don't want even to *think* about how many cold showers I've had,' he ground out, pacing angrily around the room. 'Or the times when I've had to control myself desperately, striving to behave like a reasonably civilised human being. And what thanks do I get?' he hissed savagely, spinning on his heel to face her once more. 'I return home, tired and weary, only to be told that the one and only girl I've ever really loved has suddenly taken off like a rocket. No one knows why she's disappeared. Or where she's gone. Betty has been absolutely frantic, and in tears most of the time. And as for me... Oh, my God, Angelica!' he groaned, taking a swift step forward and gathering her into his arms.

'I've been totally pole-axed by terror at what could have happened to you,' he muttered huskily, burying his face in the fragrant cloud of her newly washed, long, silky hair. 'I can't even *begin* to tell you what I've been through. The anguish of the nights, when all I could do was to pray for your safety!' His arms tightened convulsively about her trembling figure.

'I didn't mean to upset everyone...' she murmured helplessly, her mind in a complete whirl. Had he *really* said that he loved her? It seemed almost too miraculous to be true, but she was still totally confused. She'd obviously been the victim of a mountain of falsehood, but it all seemed so complicated that she didn't know where to begin trying to sort out the truth from so many lies.

'I didn't realise...I still don't understand...' She gasped as his hands swept down over her quivering body beneath the thin silk gown, lingering hungrily on the soft, warm curves of her unconfined breasts and the hard, swollen nipples aching for his touch.

He gave a shaky laugh, before swiftly scooping her up in his arms. 'For heaven's sake, Angelica! Why don't you just shut up and point me towards your bedroom?' he demanded urgently.

'You can't possibly...not here, in Kim's apartment. And it's only eleven o'clock in the morning, for heaven's sake!' she exclaimed in a shocked voice, despite being thrilled to the core by his masterly disregard of her protest, and knowing that she ought to be thoroughly ashamed of herself as she pointed towards her bedroom door.

'I have Kim's full permission to make mad, passionate love to you—all day, if necessary!' he retorted, striding swiftly into the room, and tossing her lightly down on to the bed. 'God knows, I should have done this a long time ago—and to hell with the consequences!' he added with a husky laugh, quickly stripping off his jacket.

'Luke! What on earth do you think you're doing?' she demanded, scrambling to pull her silk robe tightly about her body.

He gave another husky laugh. 'Come on, Angelica! I know that you're an old-fashioned girl, and amazingly innocent for someone of your age, but no one's *that* green! What do you think I'm going to do? Read you a goodnight story?'

'Well ... I obviously hope that you're going to—er—make love to me—even if I am a bit "innocent", as you put it,' she told him, with as much dignity as she could muster in the circumstances. 'But you still haven't explained so many things, and...'

'Explanations will have to wait,' he rasped, his voice thick with passion as he quickly joined her on the bed, gathering her quivering body tenderly into his arms. 'Frankly, my darling, I'm a hungry and desperate man,' he whispered, sweeping aside her robe to feast his eyes on her soft, glowing flesh. 'We'll talk later, but just for the moment...' his powerful frame shook with barely suppressed desire as his hands moved to caress her full breasts softly '...just let me make love to you, hmm?'

The hoarse, husky note in his voice sent shivers of excitement tingling through her body. And then, as if she'd suddenly been plunged into icy water, she realised that they faced a major problem.

'Luke!' she gasped helplessly. 'It's no good. We...we can't! I mean, what about my leg...the cast...?'

He gave a low, throaty rumble of laughter. 'My darling idiot—relax! Do you seriously imagine that I'm going to be put off by such a simple thing as one plaster cast?' he murmured, lowering his dark head for a moment to press his lips to the soft, quivering flesh on her upper thigh.

There seemed to be a strange humming noise in her ears, her heart pounding in a mad, crazy rhythm as his lips trailed slowly up over her trembling body. It was as though she'd lost all sense of time and space, only aware of the caressing touch of his hands and mouth, mindlessly responding to their sensual touch. Cupping her full breasts in his hands, he lowered his head to brush his lips tantalisingly over her taut nipples, and she found herself moaning helplessly at the sudden, thrilling ache deep in her stomach.

'Darling, Angelica,' he breathed softly, raising his head to gaze down at her. 'Don't you think that it's about time you learned to trust me, hmm . . .?'

The fierce, passionate desire in his glittering grey eyes practically took her breath away.

'Oh, Luke!' she whispered. 'How could I have been so stupid . . . or so blind? I do trust you—I really do love and trust you with all my heart,' she vowed quietly.

'No more than I love and cherish you,' he whispered against her mouth, before his lips closed over hers in a possessive hunger that thrilled her to the core.

As his hands and mouth moved sensually and erotically over her body, his soft kisses becoming more intimate and arousing, deep, husky murmurs of endearment were torn from his throat, his strong body trembling at her uninhibited and sensual response to his lovemaking.

Because she was drowning, panting for release from the almost tangible excitement and tension which seemed to fill her whole existence, it wasn't until she was nearly fainting with desire and delight that Angelica became aware of being lifting up towards him. His hard, firm manhood seemed to fill every space inside her, slowly and carefully guiding her towards a peak of excitement and joy which she could never have believed possible. An aching pleasure suddenly burst into flames deep in the innermost core of her body, and she cried out with joy, great shudders shaking her slim figure as he brought them both to the very peak of sexual fulfilment, and an overwhelming explosion of mutual love and passion.

'Is it always like that?' Angelica murmured as she lay sleepily in his arms. 'I never dreamed . . . I had no idea that making love could be quite *so* wonderful!' She sighed happily.

'Yes, it can,' he murmured, tucking a stray lock of her long, silky hair behind her ear. 'But it's very rare for two people to be so in tune with one another as you and I seem to be,' he breathed, turning his dark head to plant a kiss on her soft breast. 'How I love you, my darling!'

'I thought you didn't believe in love?' she teased happily.

He gave a muffled snort of laughter. 'What a fool I was! I thought I knew everything, didn't I? But how could I know what was going to happen to me, when I first saw a crazy-looking girl, in those outlandish clothes, trying to fool a group of tourists that she knew anything at all about the City of London?'

'I wasn't *that* bad!' she protested.

'Oh, yes,
kissed…and,
absolutely gol
happening to m
it had definitely
you again, to h
wondered if I w
I couldn't leave
you—totally and
like it. So I don't
that it was really l
lust which Norma

'However did
demanded.

IT STARTED WITH

182

'The name was easy. It
was the puzzler. In fact
Webster's company
address book.
'*What?*' Sh
staring dow
to tell m
'H
sli

. . . Angelica

'I know *everything* that goes on in my office. But, out in the everyday world, it seems that I'm more than capable of being foolishly blind, just like everyone else!'

'Well, you mustn't tell Norma that you know, or she'll think I told you. I really like her, and I wouldn't want her to be upset.'

'Yes, Norma's a pearl among women,' he agreed. 'In fact, I used her to help me find out all about you. I knew that if I rang your tour outfit they might be suspicious of a man asking for the name of a female guide. So I got Norma to do it, *and* to find out where you were next going to be, after that tour of the City.'

'You rotter!' she laughed, giving him a sharp dig in the ribs. 'That was downright sneaky of you! I nearly went mad worrying about how you'd found out my name and address.'

was the address which
, I had to buy half of David
just so I could get a look at his

raised herself up on an elbow,
at him in astonishment. 'Do you mean
e...?'

mm, I'm afraid so,' he muttered, flushing
ghtly as she glared at him. 'I seem to have spent
much of my time trying to keep tabs on you. Betty
was a great help, of course. It was she, for instance,
who told me that you were going to be at that exhibition in Leighton House, which gave me time to
organise our meal at the Ritz. And it's no good
being angry with her,' he added with a laugh,
adroitly moving aside as Angelica tried to kick him
with her heavy plaster cast, 'because, as you know,
she loves you dearly, and only wants you to be
happy. Luckily, she considers that I'm absolutely
the right person to make sure of that!'

'If I didn't love you so much, I might think that
you were an arrogant, conceited swine!' she
grumbled.

'And you'd probably be right!' he agreed with a
grin, before tenderly pressing his lips to the warm,
scented valley between her breasts. 'Quite frankly,
darling, I think I must have become almost insane
as far as you were concerned. For instance, after
I'd caught sight of you with your arms around a
tall, fair-haired man in the street, I nearly went
berserk! That's when I had to make sure that I
bought a controlling interest in Footsteps in Time,
and got you well away from any attractive men.'

She gazed ⟨...⟩
before gigglin⟨...⟩
pillows. 'Oh, y⟨...⟩
Greg, and I thin⟨...⟩
wasting your time⟨...⟩
he doesn't ... well, ⟨...⟩
if you know what I n⟨...⟩

'Ah—I may have m⟨...⟩
he admitted with a grin.⟨...⟩
having blue badge guid⟨...⟩
business anyway—I made s⟨...⟩
on you, when I was trying to ⟨...⟩ marry me.
Not that I cared a fig for that ⟨...⟩ old house, of
course, although I've now become extremely fond
of it. But *you* loved it. So, offering to take over
your burdens, and thus enabling you to continue
living there, seemed the best route to your heart.'

'But I thought ... Eleanor said ...'

'That bloody woman!' he exploded. 'I'm sorry,
darling,' he added quickly, 'but when I think of
what she tried to do to you ... I could quite cheerfully murder the evil woman!'

'I think you'd better tell me all about her, and
then ... then, maybe, we can forget she ever existed?'
Angelica asked quietly.

'The sooner we can forget her, the better I'll feel,'
he agreed grimly, before taking a deep breath. 'Well,
I'd better get it over with, I suppose, and admit
that I have, in the past, had a spasmodic affair with
Eleanor. She *never* captured my heart, as you have
so clearly done, and, if I could deny the awkward
truth, believe me I would do so. But, from the very
first moment I set eyes on you, please believe me

never been anyone else

...mured, snuggling up to his warm
...do believe you, Luke.'

...e a heavy sigh of relief. 'Unfortunately,
...hough it sounds immodest to say so, Eleanor
...n't take kindly to being so unceremoniously
dumped by me, and it now seems that she was determined to pay me back. I understand the awful
woman has a new, prestigious job in New York,
and was just making as much trouble as she could
before leaving Britain. However,' he added grimly,
'revenge is a dish best tasted cold. And, in the
fullness of time, I think that she'll find I have
blocked all her career prospects, and that she is virtually unemployable. I sincerely hope so, anyway!'

'That's a bit bloodthirsty!'

'Believe me, when I think what I'd like to do to
her, I'm being generous!' he growled. 'However,
the evil woman had a ring-side view of my unexpected inheritance, through her relationship with
that old dragon, Lady Marshall. And she used her
knowledge of my interview with the old woman to
spin a complete fabrication about my desire to oust
you from Lonsdale House.

'*Nothing* could be further from the truth,
Angelica,' he assured her with a loving kiss. 'I was
only interested in your home because it meant a
great deal to you. Which is why I tried to ''buy''
you, that day I proposed to you in the garden. I
wanted *you*, not the damn house! And that is why
I never referred to your letter, which some kind
passer-by must have picked up and put in the

postbox. Because I was deeply ashamed to discover, after your terrible accident, that it had been my possessive greed which had led to your ending up in hospital. I wanted you to love me, without any pressure, and so I decided to try and slow things down with a bit of old-fashioned courtship.

'Unfortunately, it appears that it's not something I'm very good at,' he admitted with an unhappy shrug. 'I nearly went mad with frustration at not being able to get my hands on your lovely body. And I somehow mistakenly left you feeling that I didn't care. In fact, I was planning to sweep you off your feet when I came back from New York.'

'And you have!' she told him lovingly.

But Luke was still clearly troubled by what had happened to the beautiful girl lying in his arms.

'I should have thrown that letter away, of course.' He sighed heavily. 'But it was the only letter I'd ever had from you, and so I put it away in my desk, at my apartment. And it seems I made the classic error in not demanding my keys back from Eleanor when I terminated our relationship. Because I can only assume that she must have gone to my apartment, found the letter, and used it to torture you. Believe me, boiling that wicked woman in oil would be much too good for her!'

'Oh, darling, can't we put all that behind us now?' she begged.

'You are a wonderfully generous girl, whom I love with every fibre of my being,' he murmured, turning over to give her a long, heart-stopping kiss.

'Wow!' she laughed breathlessly, when he slowly and reluctantly raised his head.

'Wow, indeed!' he agreed with a laugh. 'So, my lovely one, I hope that you are going to marry me just as soon as I can arrange a wedding?'

'Hmm ... yes, please!' she murmured happily.

'And I also hope that we'll be able to live together in that weird house of ours, growing fat on dear Betty's cooking, and surrounded by any number of children—preferably girls, looking exactly like their mother!'

'Well...*I'd* like some boys, hopefully the spitting image of their wonderful, arrogant, impossible father!' she murmured, yawning as she snuggled up to Luke's warm body.

Kim had been quite right. Angelica knew that all her future happiness was bound up with this man, and that she wanted nothing more than to spend the rest of her days with him, surrounded by children, in their lovely old house down by the river.

How incredibly lucky she was! Angelica told herself as she closed her eyes, drifting slowly asleep within the security of Luke's firm arms. It seemed almost unbelievable that so much love, passion and sheer happiness could have led from that first, shockingly unexpected but wonderfully exciting kiss!

HARLEQUIN PRESENTS®

Ever felt the excitement of a dangerous desire...?

The thrill of a feverish flirtation...?

Passion is guaranteed with the latest in our new selection of sensual stories.

Indulge in...

Dangerous Liaisons

Falling in love is a risky affair!

Coming next month:

An Unforgettable Man by Penny Jordan
Harlequin Presents #1805
"Penny Jordan pens a formidable read."
—*Romantic Times*

Who *was* Gideon Reynolds? Courage accepted him as her new boss, but Gideon also aroused her as only one other man ever had. Could they possibly be one and the same? And if Gideon *was* the unforgettable man from Courage's past...why all the secrecy?

Available in April wherever Harlequin books are sold.

MILLION DOLLAR SWEEPSTAKES
AND
EXTRA BONUS PRIZE DRAWING

No purchase necessary. To enter the sweepstakes, follow the directions published and complete and mail your Official Entry Form. If your Official Entry Form is missing, or you wish to obtain an additional one (limit: one Official Entry Form per request, one request per outer mailing envelope) send a separate, stamped, self-addressed #10 envelope (4 1/8" X 9 1/2") via first-class mail to: Million Dollar Sweepstakes and Extra Bonus Prize Drawing Entry Form, P.O. Box 1867, Buffalo, NY 14269-1867. Request must be received no later than January 15, 1998. For eligibility into the sweepstakes, entries must be received no later than March 31,1998. No liability is assumed for printing errors, lost, late, non-delivered or misdirected entries. Odds of winning are determined by the number of eligible entries distributed and received.

Sweepstakes open to residents of the U.S. (except Puerto Rico), Canada and Europe who are 18 years of age or older. All applicable laws and regulations apply. Sweepstakes offer void wherever prohibited by law. Values of all prizes are in U.S. currency. This sweepstakes is presented by Torstar Corp., its subsidiaries and affiliates, in conjunction with book, merchandise and/or product offerings. For a copy of the Official Rules governing this sweepstakes, send a self-addressed, stamped envelope (WA residents need not affix return postage) to: MILLION DOLLAR SWEEP-STAKES AND EXTRA BONUS PRIZE DRAWING Rules, P.O. Box 4470, Blair, NE 68009-4470, USA.

FAST CASH 4033 DRAW RULES
NO PURCHASE OR OBLIGATION NECESSARY

Fifty prizes of $50 each will be awarded in random drawings to be conducted no later than 6/28/96 from amongst all eligible responses to this prize offer received as of 5/14/96. To enter, follow directions, affix 1st-class postage and mail OR write Fast Cash 4033 on a 3" x 5" card along with your name and address and mail that card to: Harlequin's Fast Cash 4033 Draw, P.O. Box 1395, Buffalo, NY 14240-1395 OR P.O. Box 618, Fort Erie, Ontario L2A 5X3. (Limit: one entry per outer envelope; all entries must be sent via 1st-class mail.) Limit: one prize per household. Odds of winning are determined by the number of eligible responses received. Offer is open only to residents of the U.S. (except Puerto Rico) and Canada and is void wherever prohibited by law. All applicable laws and regulations apply. Any litigation within the province of Quebec respecting the conduct and awarding of a prize in this sweepstakes may be submitted to the Régie des alcools, des courses et des jeux. In order for a Canadian resident to win a prize, that person will be required to correctly answer a time-limited arithmetical skill-testing question to be administered by mail. Names of winners available after 7/30/96 by sending a self-addressed, stamped envelope to: Fast Cash 4033 Draw Winners, P.O. Box 4200, Blair, NE 68009-4200.

SWP-H3ZD

HARLEQUIN  PRESENTS®

brings you
Sandra Field's exciting new trilogy:

*First they were strangers, then they were
lovers, now they're Significant Others!*

Starting in April, we'll be bringing you a brand-new
three-part series by bestselling author Sandra Field that
celebrates the magical mayhem of modern relationships
and the dating game. Watch for:

Beyond Reach

Troy Donovan was tough, uncompromising, and had no
intention of letting anyone get close to him again. But as
far as Lucy was concerned she would make her own rules.
He'd told her he didn't believe in mixing business with
pleasure...and that was fine with Lucy. Why let business
get in the way of anything?

Each of Sandra's books can be read on its own, but why
not follow Lucy and Troy's story in *Second Honeymoon*,
out in August?

And next year Lucy's sister Marcia finds her own
significant other in *After Hours*—coming soon from
Harlequin Presents!

Sandra Field's books are *"Pure pleasure..."*
—*Romantic Times*

Where there's a will there's a way...
for four charismatic characters to find true love

by Sandra Marton

When Charles Landon dies, he leaves behind a different
legacy for each of his children.

As Cade, Grant, Zach and Kyra react to the terms of
their father's will, each receives an unexpected yet
delightful bequest:

A very special love affair that will last a lifetime!

Watch for:

> Cade's story: *An Indecent Proposal*—
> Harlequin Presents #1808—April 1996
>
> Grant's story: *Guardian Groom*—
> Harlequin Presents #1813—May 1996
>
> Zach's story: *Hollywood Wedding*—
> Harlequin Presents #1819—June 1996
>
> Kyra's story: *Spring Bride*—
> Harlequin Presents #1825—July 1996

Harlequin Presents—you'll want to know what
happens next!

Available wherever Harlequin books are sold.

Yo amo novelas con corazón!

Starting this March, Harlequin opens up to a whole new world of readers with two new romance lines in SPANISH!

Harlequin Deseo
* passionate, sensual and exciting stories

Harlequin Bianca
* romances that are fun, fresh and very contemporary

With four titles a month, each line will offer the same wonderfully romantic stories that you've come to love—now available in Spanish.

Look for them at selected retail outlets.

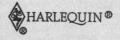

HARLEQUIN ®

You're About to Become a *Privileged Woman*

Reap the rewards of fabulous free gifts and benefits with proofs-of-purchase from Harlequin and Silhouette books

Pages & Privileges™

It's our way of thanking you for buying our books at your favorite retail stores.

Harlequin and Silhouette— the most privileged readers in the world!

For more information about Harlequin and Silhouette's PAGES & PRIVILEGES program call the Pages & Privileges Benefits Desk: 1-503-794-2499

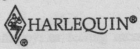

HARLEQUIN®